WHAT'S WRONG WITH Rusty?

HEATHER Grovet

REVIEW AND HERALD® PUBLISHING ASSOCIATION
HAGERSTOWN, MD 21740

The author assumes full responsibility for the accuracy of all facts and quotations as cited in this book.

This book was
Edited by Jeannette R. Johnson
Designed by Square 1 Design
Interior design by Candy Harvey
Cover illustration by Marcus Mashburn
Typeset: Century Schoolbook 13/16

PRINTED IN U.S.A.
08 07 06 05 04   5 4 3 2 1

R&H Cataloging Service
Grovet, Heather Marie, 1963-
     What's wrong with Rusty?

     I. Title.

                    813.6

ISBN 0-8280-1756-5

Other books by Heather Grovet:

Petunia, the Ugly Pug
Prince Prances Again
Prince, the Persnickety Pony
Sarah Lee and a Mule Named Maybe
Marvelous Mark and His No-good Dog

To order, call 1-800-765-6955.
     Visit us at www.reviewandherald.com for information on other Review and Herald® products.

CONTENTS

1

A DUMB THING HAPPENS TO SMART ME

OK, so I was dumb. Dense.

I admit it.

I'm a smart 12-year-old, but even smart 12-year-olds do a few dumb things. This was one of them.

And it wasn't all my fault.

My dad says that I wasn't dumb. OK—he says I *was* dumb, but he also said, "This winter was an important growth experience for you."

"A growth experience?" I had groaned. "What's that supposed to mean?"

"It means that God had something important to teach you," Dad continued with a grin. "And sometimes the only way you seem to learn is by hitting your head on a brick wall a few dozen times."

That wasn't very nice, was it? And my dad's a pastor, so you'd think he'd be nice all the

time—at least to his kids! I suppose there was
some truth to Dad's comment. I did have a lot
of things I needed to learn about God. And
about me.

You know, before all this happened I
thought I could do anything. I could take care
of myself. I was tough. I was strong. I was
healthy. I was—OK, you get the point.

God didn't seem that important in my life.
Don't get me wrong—I loved God, and all. But
in some ways He seemed like a fairy godmother who appeared now and then to rescue
me. If I needed something I could make a
wish, and *poof!* God would make it happen.
Other than that, I didn't need Him. I thought
I could take care of myself.

Boy, did I have a lot to learn!

And it all started in school.

I had been having problems for a few
weeks, and my teacher, Mrs. Rodney, was getting a bad attitude about the whole thing.

All I had done was raise my hand in the air.

Mrs. Rodney didn't even wait to see what I
needed. Instead, she glared at me. "What do
you need, Rusty?" she asked. Her whole face
frowned at me: her chin was down, her eyebrows were down, and her mouth was most
definitely turned down.

I squirmed in my seat, hesitating. But

there are some things that wait for no one—not even teachers. This was one of them.

"I have to go to the bathroom," I said.

The girl across from me giggled, but I ignored her.

"The bathroom?" Mrs. Rodney asked pointedly. "Again?"

"Yes," I said, feeling my face begin to tingle. "The bathroom."

This was embarrassing. I mean, maybe Mrs. Rodney would just like to get on the intercom and notify the entire school. *Attention, please. I wish to announce that Craig Michael Hill needs to go to the bathroom. Again.*

"I don't believe you," Mrs. Rodney said.

"Honest," I said, feeling my face begin to get hot. "I have to go."

Mrs. Rodney gave me one more glare for good measure, and then jabbed her finger toward the door. "Go!" she said. "But this will be the last time."

Her eyes sizzled as I slunk to the classroom door. *I don't know what you're up to,* they seemed to say, *but I intend to find out.*

I shut the door quietly behind me and hurried down the long hallway. I could feel my ears tingling like they do when I get embarrassed. First, my forehead turns red, then my whole face, and last—but certainly not least—

are my ears. They turn bright-red. Fire-engine red. Rudolph-the-red-nosed-reindeer red.

You get the picture.

Oh, and don't forget my matching red hair. My dad has auburn hair, and I guess I take after him. But you could never say mine is auburn. Every single hair on my head is flaming red. Even my eyebrows and eyelashes are red. And yes, I have freckles, so I positively glow in the dark when I blush. Red cheeks, red ears, and red neck underneath my shock of bright-red hair.

Hayden Granger, the class clown, calls me Tomato Head. He says that if I turn any redder I'll burst open like an overripe tomato. (Sounds messy, doesn't it?) Anyway, who's Hayden trying to impress? With a name like Hayden, he should hardly be making jokes about other people.

Anyway, I won't get started on Hayden. Let's get back to my problem.

Mrs. Rodney was wrong. I wasn't trying to fool her. The last thing I wanted to do was embarrass myself and go to the bathroom. I wasn't looking for trouble, and I wasn't trying to get out of class.

But something was wrong with me, and I didn't know what.

That's why I told you I was dumb. I mean,

how could anyone have a serious problem like mine and not know what that problem was? I nearly died a few days later, and I didn't even know what was happening! I guess that's because I didn't know a thing about—

Whoops!

Didn't mean to tell you that! I'm getting ahead of myself. Forget I said anything about dying. It's going to ruin my whole story, and I wouldn't want that to happen. You know, there's nothing worse than reading a really good book, and being in such a rush to find out what happens that you skip to the last page.

I did that once this year, and it ruined everything. There wasn't any use finishing the book, because I already knew that the hero survived the plane crash and lived in the forest for months, eating rabbits and birds.

I just about did that to you, and you haven't even skipped to the back of this book yet. So I'm sorry. Forget about it.

Now where was I? Oh, yes, I was rushing to the washroom.

Mrs. Rodney was wrong.

I *did* have to go to the bathroom. I'd been going an awful lot that month. Once I had begun to tell my mother about it, but then I stopped. A person's private affairs are private, after all. Who wants to talk to their parents

about going to the bathroom? For sure not me. And what was I going to say, anyway? That I was spending "quality time" every recess, and at noon, in that little room—and still I had to leave class sometimes to go again? That's why Mrs. Rodney was so mad at me. She couldn't believe that anyone would have to go that often.

My hockey coach was annoyed with me, too. Last week I had left in the middle of hockey practice to make a quick trip to the bathroom. "Right in the middle of our power play," Coach Wilson had grumbled. I couldn't help it. Power play, or no power play.

I was dense. I admit it.

But Mrs. Rodney was wrong about one thing.

I may have been dense, but I wasn't dishonest.

I'm a preacher's kid, and I can't afford to be dishonest. Especially since I go to public school now. (There's no church school anywhere remotely close to where we live.) Teachers always seem to have one eye on preacher's kids anyway, just waiting for them to do something wrong.

Now I want you to know that I'm a pretty decent kid. I clean my room and do most of my homework, and I don't get into very many fights.

I listen to my parents, and I'm nice to my

sister—OK, I guess I'm taking things a little bit beyond the believable.

Sorry. My point is, I wasn't a troublemaker as Mrs. Rodney seemed to think.

I just had to go to the bathroom too often.

After this latest trip to the washroom, I stopped at the water fountain and sucked up some big gulps of ice-cold water. I knew it wasn't smart to drink again, but I couldn't help myself. Something was screaming inside me: "Drink, drink, drink!"

So I did.

Then I wiped the drops of water off my face and slid back into my classroom. I did my best to ignore Mrs. Rodney and her frowning face. I picked up my pencil and flipped the pages in my math book.

Three thousand and twelve divided by 18.

That was easy.

I wrote the numbers on my paper and began to work. But before long another familiar feeling began in the pit of my stomach.

My stomach began to rumble and groan. I was nauseated, and a bit dizzy, too. That was something else that had been happening a lot lately.

It's probably just the flu, I told myself, flipping a page in my notebook. I remembered how horrible I had felt last month when I'd

caught a nasty bug from my older sister, Jessica. I'd been violently sick to my stomach for two entire days, and later I developed a horrible cough. I'd finally quit coughing, but my stomach had bothered me ever since.

At least I wasn't so sick anymore. I closed my eyes for a moment, remembering how horrible I had felt last month.

"I'll bet you gave me the flu on purpose!" I'd yelled at Jessica as I bent over the toilet, puking.

"That's right," Jessica had shot back. "Just consider it my birthday present to you, dear brother."

Lucky, lucky me. I'd spent my twelfth birthday throwing up in the bathroom. And the only one in my house who had seemed worried about me was my cat, Pumpkin. Dad was at work, and Jessica just locked herself in her room, hollering, "Keep your stupid germs away from me!" And Mom, well, she wasn't much help, either. Oh, she brought me some medicine (which did absolutely no good), and she wiped my face with a cool cloth once or twice. Otherwise, she fussed around the house, only peeking in every so often to see if I was alive or dead.

So I guess it was a good thing that I had Pumpkin. For some reason, Pumpkin must

have decided that he was my official nurse, because he spent those two days lying on my chest, purring. It was nice, in an uncomfortable sort of way, except my bed got covered by orange cat hairs, and Mom had been grumpy when she'd changed my sheets.

But now I should be feeling better. Rugged men like me don't get sick. I opened my eyes and tried to concentrate on my math. The numbers in front of me wobbled back and forth, and I blinked, trying to bring them back into focus.

I felt horrible. My head ached, and my stomach ached, and I was suddenly so tired I could hardly keep my eyes open.

I yawned, and blinked my eyes again.

The classroom clock's numbers swam in front of my eyes. I squinted, and the numbers finally arranged themselves in order. It was 3:20. Only 10 minutes until school was out for the day. I had hockey practice after supper.

I'm not ashamed to admit that all I really wanted to do was go home and climb into bed. That's nothing to be ashamed of, is it? Everyone has a breaking point. I was tough, but even tough guys can break.

I'll bet you'd have climbed under the covers, too, if you'd have felt as awful as I did.

13

WHO'S COMING TO
OUR HOUSE?

Rusty!" Mom called.

I groaned and sat up on the couch. "What?"

"Coach Wilson just phoned," Mom said. "Hockey practice has been canceled until Thursday."

"Good," I said. The smell of supper wafted around the living room corner and filled my nostrils. I inhaled deeply. Something smelled delicious. In fact, I realized that I wasn't nauseated anymore. Instead, I was hungry.

"Good?" Mom frowned. "Don't you like hockey anymore?"

I stretched on the couch. "I love hockey," I said. "But I just didn't feel like going tonight."

A sudden *thud* on my chest made me grunt loudly. Stupid cat! Pumpkin was an enormous cat now, heavier than any of my friends' wimpy cats (maybe even bigger than some of

their dogs), but in Pumpkin's mind he was still a little kitten. And now that not-so-little "kitten" was perched cheerfully on my chest, a wide smile on his cat face.

"Boy, have you got bad breath," I grumbled, shoving the cat to the side. "What did you have for dinner—fried rat?"

Pumpkin may not be very smart, but he's loyal. He immediately scrambled back to sit on me again. He purred louder than ever, his round cat face twinkling at me. Pumpkin rubbed his moist nose against my chin, and then turned around once or twice to settle back on my chest.

"Thanks a lot, Pumpkin," I groaned. "Your breath was bad enough. Now you've got the other end squashed up against my face." Pumpkin twitched his tail against my nose, making me hold my breath.

"I'd be sick now if I hadn't been before this!" I said, giving Pumpkin another shove off the couch. I rolled over with a groan.

Wow! It would be nice to be as secure as a cat. If someone gave me a shove off the couch, especially two times in a row, I'd catch the hint. I'd probably have my feelings hurt and sulk all day. Of course, boys don't sulk, but I'd have been aloof. Cool. Distant.

But not Pumpkin. He landed on the floor

with a firm thump (he's not the most graceful cat in the world), then immediately sprang back onto the couch. A second later, Pumpkin was back on my lap, purring contentedly.

Like I said, Pumpkin was dumb but loyal. It was almost as though he assumed he'd fallen off my lap by accident.

No one would ever want to get rid of me, his bright-yellow eyes beamed. *I'm such a lovable guy.*

A stinky, heavy, lovable guy.

The front door suddenly burst open, and Jessica and my dad bounded inside. Well, Jessica bounded, and my dad followed at a more adult-like pace. But they were both grinning, and I knew Jessica had something to announce even before she opened her big mouth.

"Guess what?" she whooped. "Ryan Smith is coming to supper tomorrow!"

"Ryan who?" Mom asked.

"Ryan Smith," Jessica repeated. She dramatically clasped her hands and looked soulfully toward the sky.

"Who's Ryan Smith?" Mom asked.

Dad flopped down on the couch and beamed at me. "Only the number one left wing for the Edmonton Oilers," he said. He ran his fingers through my short red hair, spiking it up at the front.

"The Edmonton Oilers?" I asked.

"Yes, the Oilers," Dad said.

I stared at him and didn't say anything.

Jessica swooned in the background. "The Edmonton Oilers," she said. "You know, the hockey team. You do watch hockey, don't you, Rusty?"

I gave my head a shake. "The Edmonton Oilers?"

Dad laughed. "I think we surprised him, Jessica," he said. "Don't you?"

Well, I wouldn't say I was surprised, exactly. I would say amazed. Dumbfounded. Shocked. In fact, my first thought was *I must be dreaming!*

"Ryan Smith!" Jessica sighed. "He's so good-looking."

Girls! What's with them?

"Ryan Smith's not good-looking," I said. "He's a hockey player!"

"A good-looking hockey player," Jessica corrected me. "And he's coming to eat with us."

"What's this all about?" Mom asked. She gave my father a suspicious look. "Were you at the rink today, Raymond?"

"No, Carol," Dad said. "I spent the entire day working at the church office. Although I have to admit that a lap or two on the ice would have felt good."

17

"So why do we have a hockey player coming to our house for supper tomorrow?" Mom asked.

"It's a long story," Dad said. "Ryan Smith's younger brother, Kelly, is friends with Mrs. Cullen's son, Sid."

"Who?"

"You know, Mrs. Cullen. The lady who cleans the church," Dad continued. "Ryan will be in town tomorrow playing a hockey game, and Sid invited Kelly and Ryan over for supper. I guess they said yes."

"So why are they coming here, to our house?" I asked.

"Mrs. Cullen said no," Dad said. "She has an appointment that evening with her accountant, or some such thing."

"She'd rather see her accountant than a hockey star?" I gasped in disbelief.

"Anyhow," Dad went on smoothly, "I told the poor woman that we'd be willing to feed a couple extra men." He paused and looked at Mom. "If that's OK with you, honey."

Mom smiled. "I wondered if you were going to ask," she said.

"'Do not forget to entertain strangers,'" I began to recite, "'for . . . some people have entertained angels without knowing it.' Hebrews 13, verse 2, New International Version."

Mom looked at me and raised her eyebrows.

"New International Version?" she asked.

"Last week's memory verse," I said quickly. "See? I was paying attention."

"Well, I've got one for you," she replied with a small smirk. "Proverbs 6, verse 9, King James Version. Read it."

"I don't have time to read the Bible right now!" I yelled. "We need to make some plans— Ryan Smith is coming for supper tomorrow!"

"I think it has finally sunk into his thick skull!" Jessica observed.

Thick skull? Why, if I wasn't such a polite guy I'd have found an appropriate comment about Jessica's skull. But while I was thinking as fast as humanly possible, Mom came up with something of her own to say.

"I just don't know," Mom said. Her voice was hesitant. "I may need to see our accountant, too."

"Mom!"

A shot of horror knifed through my body. What was with adults needing to see their accountants?

"Tell me you're kidding!" Jessica said. Her voice was desperate.

I was desperate. And cool 12-year-old boys don't get desperate very often. But this was a desperate situation, that's for sure.

"I'm kidding," Mom laughed. "I guess we

can find enough food to feed a couple more people."

I sucked in a deep breath. I think it was the first breath I had taken in the last minute or so. I had never suspected my mother of being so cruel. To torment me like that, to suggest that Ryan Smith wouldn't be able to come to our place—it was too much to believe. It's a good thing I'm a tough person, because a lot of other guys I know probably would have passed out right then and there on the kitchen floor. Especially if they were as sick as I'd been lately.

"They'll be big people," Dad warned. "Ryan Smith is a big man, and I expect he'll have a good appetite."

"Big or small, I'm sure we'll manage," Mom said, smiling back.

Jessica and I let out screams of joy. Pumpkin's ears flattened back, and finally he got to his feet and slunk out of the room.

I didn't really notice. All I could see was Jessica bouncing around as though she was on a berserk pogo stick. And I wasn't far behind her.

"Come on," Mom called. "Let's eat before the soup scorches."

"We wouldn't notice the difference," I teased. "We're used to 'burnt offerings.'"

"Watch it, buster," Mom said, grinning back at me.

"Some people ring the dinner bell," I told the rest of the family, "but Mom lets us know when it's time to eat by setting off the smoke detector."

Mom reached over and gave me a playful whack on the shoulder. At least I think it was playful. Mom can hit pretty hard for a woman her age!

I ate two enormous bowls of homemade vegetable soup and three buttery buns before I began to fill up. The soup wasn't burned, of course, and the buns were perfect—golden and crisp on the outside, and soft and melt-in-your-mouth tender on the inside.

My stomach was feeling 100 percent better now, and when I carefully shook my head I noticed with satisfaction that my headache was gone, too.

At bedtime I opened my Bible and looked up the verse Mom had given me before supper. It took me a few minutes to find Proverbs—I can never remember if it comes before, or after, Psalms. But I finally found the right spot.

Proverbs 6, verse 9 . . . *How long wilt thou sleep, O sluggard? when wilt thou arise out of thy sleep?*

My mom. A real comedian.

I smiled in spite of myself and shut the Bible with a satisfying smack. *God, please help me feel OK tomorrow. I don't have time to be sick. Not when Ryan Smith is coming to visit!*

I could hardly wait to tell the guys at school.

"No way!" Hayden Granger exclaimed the next morning. "Why would Ryan Smith visit a tomato head like you?"

"Drop dead, Hayden," my best friend Brett retorted. Then he looked back at me. "Why *would* Ryan Smith visit you?"

I tried to hold back my grin. "It's all because of Mrs. Cullen's accountant."

"Huh?"

"Don't ask," I said. "You'd have to be a grown-up to understand, I guess. But isn't that great? Maybe I can even get his autograph."

"That's not great," Brett said. "That's *fantabulous!* That's *incredible!* That's *awesome!* I can hardly believe it. You're not pulling my leg, are you?"

"It's the truth," I said.

"Take a photo of Ryan," Brett instructed. "With him standing beside you."

"You'll probably bust the camera," Hayden said. "Or cause a glare with that hair of yours."

I ignored Hayden and closed my eyes for a

moment, imagining the evening. There was Ryan Smith and me, side by side, posing for the picture. He would be wearing his hockey jersey, and maybe even holding a hockey stick. We'd lean together, and the flash would go off. *Hockey legend Ryan Smith poses with future hockey star, Rusty Hill.*

"You *have* to invite me over," Brett begged.

"I can't," I said. "My parents already told me: 'No extra people.'"

"Please!"

I shook my head. "No."

"Ah, you're just making this up," Hayden Granger said. "There's no way you're going to meet one of the Oilers."

"I am too," I retorted.

"Better bring the picture, Tomato Head," Hayden said. "I won't believe it until I can see it with my own eyes."

The school bell rang, and Brett quickly gathered his books from our locker. He turned to hurry down the hallway, then looked back at me. "Please!" he begged one more time.

"I can't, Brett," I said. "Honest."

Brett stared back at me. "Well, your mom had better make a really fancy supper," he called. "Maybe a big, thick steak or two. Superstars like Ryan Smith are used to eating the very best, you know."

I stopped in midstride. Steak! My family are all vegetarians. There wouldn't be any fancy steak for Ryan Smith. In fact, there probably wouldn't be anything that he'd want to eat for supper!

Suddenly I pictured the scene.

Ryan Smith would take one look at our meal, and he'd get to his feet. "Take me to the steak house," he'd say. He'd drive away, and that would be the end of all my dreams!

His autograph, the photo of us together; it all depended on one thing. A good meal.

My stomach began to knot and twist again. I wasn't sure if it was nerves or my flu, but I groaned out loud. I couldn't be sick today. I had too much to do.

When school was over, I rushed home as quickly as possible. Mom was at the kitchen counter, mixing an enormous pitcher of juice.

I reached around Mom and filled a glass full of cold water. I gulped it down quickly, then refilled the glass.

"What are we having for supper?" I asked hopefully, sniffing the air.

"Vegetarian lasagna," Mom said. "Can't you smell it cooking?"

I groaned. "Vegetarian lasagna? We can't eat that."

"Why not?"

"We need something special for Ryan Smith," I said.

"My lasagna *is* special," Mom said. She plopped some ice cubes into the pitcher and set it in the fridge.

I finished my second glass of water in a few quick swallows. "It's vegetarian," I protested. "Ryan Smith won't like it."

"Sure he will," Mom said with a faint smile. "And I have lots of other food to go with it. Garlic bread and salad and corn. No one will need to go away hungry."

"But Ryan Smith is *special*," I said.

"Everyone's special," Mom sighed. "And I try to be a good host to everyone who visits us. I'm sure Mr. Smith will enjoy his meal tonight."

I opened my mouth to argue, then closed it again.

"I'm not going to burn supper," Mom assured me. Her eyes sparkled, but I didn't smile back.

Mothers.

Didn't she realize that my entire happiness depended upon this meal?

I decided I'd better take this opportunity to go to the bathroom. There was no way I was getting up from the supper table to make the trip when Ryan Smith was sitting beside me. That would be too embarrassing.

I rushed down the hallway and into the bathroom. I washed my hands and ran my fingers through my hair. It looked horrible, as usual. I have thick hair, "thick as fleas on a dog," my dad says. I had been getting it cut really short lately, hoping that it would lie better. It didn't. Now it stands straight on end all the time. Jessica says it looks like I just finished watching a horror movie. Ha, ha! Pastor Hill's family would never watch horror movies. In fact, the only thing that resembles a horror movie around here is Jessica!

Anyhow, I wet my comb and tried to force my hair into place. Finally, I gave up and flung the comb onto the counter. "I'd be better off bald," I groaned.

Just then Pumpkin strode into the bathroom. He rubbed against my ankles, nearly tripping me as I reached for my toothbrush.

"Get outta the way, cat," I muttered, my mouth full of toothpaste. "Can't ya see I'm in a hurry?"

Pumpkin meowed once and sprang onto the rim of the toilet. He sniffed daintily, then began to lap out of the toilet.

"Eeeuuwww!" I said, shoving the cat off the toilet. "No wonder you stink all the time!"

Pumpkin's tail twitched, and he glared at

me for a moment before bouncing back onto the toilet seat.

"That's it," I said. I set my toothbrush down with a damp *thwap* and grabbed Pumpkin in my arms. The moment I picked him up, the cat began to purr.

Well, now, you've finally come to your senses, Pumpkin seemed to say. He pressed his big paws against my neck in a bear hug—uhhh, in a cat hug, you might say.

I didn't take the time to hug Pumpkin back. Instead, I opened the door to the basement and tossed him down the steps.

That sounds horrible, doesn't it?

What I mean to say is that I set Pumpkin on the basement steps (rather quickly, I might add), and then slammed the door behind him. "Drink out of your cat dish," I called to my pet, wiping short orange hair off my navy sweatshirt. "That's what it's for, you know."

Dad and Jessica came home a few minutes later.

"I'll set the table," Jessica yelled. She rushed across the kitchen and flung the china cabinet door open. In a few minutes a pile of good china and crystal goblets appeared on our table.

"You don't fool me," I said. "You must be an impostor. My real sister would never do a job without being forced."

27

"Very funny." Jessica glared at me and began to gather a stack of plates. "Like you're Mr. Hard Worker yourself."

"I do a lot more chores than you do," I retorted.

"Right." Jessica sneered and began to set the dishes around the table neatly. "In that case, pass me the good silverware, slave boy."

"What good silverware?"

"The only good silverware we own, Einstein," Jessica said.

"Why?"

Jessica groaned and shook her head. "So the table looks nice," she said.

"Thank you for thinking of me," I said, rummaging in the cupboard for the box of silverware. "It's nice to know you care."

"This isn't for *you!* You can eat in the bathroom, for all I care," Jessica snapped. "It's Ryan Smith who matters."

Dad frowned and held a big hand up in the air. "Quiet, you two!"

I didn't quit. I fluffed my hair and tilted my shoulders back and minced on tiptoes over to the table, carrying the silverware. "Oh, Ryan," I cooed. "You big, handsome man. Sit here close to me and I'll help you cut your food. See? It's our good silverware!"

"Cut it out!" Jessica said. She thumped the

stack of plates on the table.

I didn't. "Why, can't you sit a little closer to me, you big strong hockey player!"

"Stop it!"

"And Ryan, what big blue eyes you have," I sighed dramatically, blinking my eyes rapidly at Jessica.

Her face flushed bright-red, and her eyes narrowed. She smacked a plate down and opened her mouth to answer me.

But Dad spoke first. "Enough!" he barked. "I don't want to hear another word out of the two of you."

"Nor do I," Mom added. "And that's pretty expensive china you're banging on the table right now."

"I'm concerned about the china," Dad said, "but that's not the biggest problem. It's their manners that worry me."

"Or lack of manners," Mom corrected.

Now that hurt. Yes, Jessica has problems with her manners, but I had thought it would be obvious to everyone else that my manners were perfect. Awesome. Impeccable.

"I don't want you fighting this evening," Dad said. "You'll ruin supper for our company." He looked at Jessica first, and then turned to face me.

"You don't need to worry," I said quickly. "I

29

won't fight. But I can't promise what Jessica will do."

Mom snorted but didn't say anything.

Jessica glared at me, and then finished setting the dishes on the table. When she was finished, she peered around intently. "Don't you have any cloth napkins?" she asked with a groan, looking at our paper napkins. "These are awful."

"Hockey players don't need napkins," I said.

"Maybe not," Jessica snapped, "but you do. In fact, you could use a bib!"

"Didn't you two hear me?" Dad asked. "I'm serious. If you fight one more time you're both going to your rooms for the evening. Then you won't have to worry about napkins or anything else."

"I can't miss supper," I said quickly. "In fact, I've got to eat soon. My stomach is beginning to feel awful again."

"Rusty!" Mom said. She looked up from the salad. "You've been sick all week."

"I'm not exactly sick," I said. "I'm just starving to death."

"Then don't forget what I just told you," Dad said. He looked at Jessica and me with a frown.

"What?" Jessica asked innocently.

The sound of a car pulling up outside made me forget all about my stomach.

"It's Ryan Smith!" Jessica exclaimed. She ran to the mirror and fluffed her hair quickly. "Do I look OK?" she asked.

"You're wasting your time," I said. Then I snapped my mouth shut and glanced sideways at Dad. He was glaring at me, so I thought quickly and revised my statement. "Ah, you're wasting your time," I continued lamely. "You already look fine." And she did, although I'd rather eat an earthworm than tell her that. Jessica's a decent-looking girl, for a sister. Somehow the red hair gene looked just right on her. She has pretty brown hair with streaks of red in it, just the color some people pay money to have their hairdresser do for them.

"I have a memory verse for you two," Dad said. His mouth twitched up at one corner, but his face remained stern. "Proverbs 25, verse 24: 'It is better to dwell in the corner of the housetop, than with a brawling woman and in a wide house.' And that's where you two are going to be if you fight again—at the corner of the housetop."

"It says a brawling woman," I pointed out, "not a brawling boy."

"Rusty!"

"Dad," Jessica said, "you don't have to worry. We're not going to fight."

"Good," Dad said. "Now, let's see if you can remember that."

31

3

RYAN SMITH EATS OUR FOOD

I hadn't seen Sid Cullen since he'd gone away to college, and I hardly recognized him. He's always been tall, but now he seemed downright enormous! But the two men who stood on either side of him were even bigger!

"Hello, Pastor Hill, Mrs. Hill," Sid said.

"Come on in," Dad invited, motioning with his hands for the men to follow. "It's too cold to stand outside on the doorstep."

The three men stepped inside and knocked the snow off their boots. "This is my friend Kelly Smith and his older brother, Ryan," Sid said.

The men shook Mom's and Dad's hands politely.

"It's nice to meet you," Ryan Smith said. His voice was deep and smooth. "We would like to thank you for inviting us over this evening."

"I hope you're hungry," Mom said with a smile.

"I always have room for a home-cooked meal," Ryan grinned.

"These are our children," Dad said. "This is Jessica, who's 15, and our son, Rusty, who turned 12 last month."

"They look just like you, Pastor Hill," Kelly Smith said.

"They've got my hair, for sure," Dad agreed, "although maybe they didn't inherit my sweet personality!"

Jessica groaned. "Please don't tell me that I look like Rusty," she said. "I mean, look at his hair—"

Dad glared at Jessica, and she suddenly became silent.

Ryan Smith looked me. He looked at my red hair, which was standing on end, I was pretty sure, and smiled. "Happy belated birthday, Rusty," he said. "And I think your hair looks fine. It's unique."

I smiled back, feeling my cheeks begin to flush. *Don't blush; don't blush!* I ordered myself, turning away from the group. I would rather disappear into a puff of smoke than blush and turn into an overripe tomato in front of these men.

I could feel myself turning redder and red-

der. My face would soon crack, and then burst, and tomato juice would ooze everywhere . . .

Stop it! I told myself. I forced a smile at the group and ran my fingers over my hair. Hopefully it wasn't too messy.

Jessica touched her own hair with one hand and fluttered her eyelashes.

"Would you like to sit down?" Dad asked, gesturing toward the living room.

The men had barely gotten settled when the oven timer rang.

"Time to eat," Mom called.

Jessica rushed to the table in a very unlady-like manner and managed to be seated beside Ryan Smith. I ended up across the table from him, seated between his brother, Kelly, and Sid Cullen. I felt very small as I sat there between two enormous men, and I pulled my shoulders close together so we weren't so crowed.

"I hope no one's left-handed," Mom said as she set the food on the table.

"Left-handed?" Dad asked, looking puzzled.

"There isn't going to be much room for maneuvering your fork," Mom laughed. "Especially if your elbows are poking your neighbor in the ribs."

"I think we'll be fine," Ryan Smith said. He playfully nudged Jessica with an elbow. "I can probably manage this little girl here."

Jessica smiled and fluttered her eyelashes again.

"Sid, would you say grace?" Dad asked when everyone was settled.

Sid prayed for us, and then we began to pass the food around the table.

The meal went very well. Ryan had two large helpings of lasagna and seemed impressed to learn that it didn't have any meat in it.

"Not even a little bit?" he asked.

Mom shook her head.

"Well, it was delicious," Ryan said, finishing his last bite of garlic bread. "My compliments for an excellent meal."

"I hope you all have room for some apple crisp," Mom said, gathering up dirty dishes. Jessica sprang to her feet and began to carefully pick up the stack of plates in front of Ryan Smith.

"*I* have room for dessert," I said.

Dad laughed. "I can hardly believe how much you're eating these days, Rusty," he said. "At this rate you're going to be bigger than the Smith brothers!"

I looked at the men who towered over me. "I don't think that would be possible," I said.

"Rusty grows sideways, not tall," Jessica said.

"Pardon me?" Ryan Smith asked.

"Fat," Jessica said.

I glared at Jessica. "Actually," I said, rubbing my stomach, "I think I lost some weight this month."

"Impossible!" Mom said. "You eat like a horse."

"More like a pig!" Jessica said tartly.

Dad frowned from across the room. "Ah, Jessica," he said, "perhaps you could go to the corner of the housetop and bring us back a pail of ice cream, OK?"

Jessica sprang to her feet with a guilty expression. "Sure, Dad," she said quickly.

I smiled to myself. *He shoots; he scores! One for me; zero for Jessica.*

Sid Cullen turned to his two friends. "Did you know that Pastor Hill used to be a hockey player?" he asked. "He was drafted in the minor leagues."

"Really?" Ryan's eyes lit up. "I didn't know that."

"It was a long time ago," Dad said modestly.

Jessica returned with the pail of vanilla ice cream, and Dad began to scoop generous spoonfuls onto the apple crisp.

"You played left wing, didn't you?" Sid continued.

Dad nodded. "But not quite as well as Ryan does."

"You're being modest," Sid scolded. "I'm told you were very good."

"I have always enjoyed hockey," Dad said. "I still play on a local rec. team. I think the exercise is good for me, especially since my job involves a lot of sitting."

"How did you end up being a minister?" Kelly Smith asked.

Dad returned to his seat and tipped his chair back a few inches. He thought for a moment. "Well," he said, "it's a long story. But I'll try to give you the short version."

Everyone turned to look at Dad.

"I became a Christian while I was at college," Dad said. "Actually, it all happened about the same time I was drafted."

The men nodded their heads.

"I started playing hockey with the farm team," Dad said. "But at the same time, I felt that God had another plan for me. The more I read my Bible, the more I felt God was calling me to the ministry."

"God spoke to you?" Ryan asked.

Dad smiled. "I told you it was a long story."

"Did you actually hear a voice speak to you?" Sid asked.

Dad slowly shook his head. "No, I wouldn't say I heard a voice," he said. "But I had a strong impression that God had other plans

for me, plans that didn't involve hockey. I prayed about it and read the Bible, and I talked to a few friends whom I respected."

"Is hockey such a bad thing?" Ryan Smith asked. He studied Dad's face seriously.

"Oh, no," Dad said quickly. "Hockey wasn't the problem. I could have been doing a million other things—working in an office or fighting fires or whatever. But if God had another plan for me I wanted to follow it, and not my own. I felt I had two choices: I could do things my way and play hockey, or I could do what God wanted and be a pastor."

"Christians can play hockey," I put in quickly.

Dad nodded his head. "Of course they can," he said. "But that wasn't God's specific plan for *me*. And although giving up hockey was very difficult, I can honestly say that I've never regretted it."

"I would," I said. Then I flushed red and put my hand over my mouth.

"That's one of my goals," Dad said with a faint smile. "I always want to follow God's plan for me. And I hope that I can teach my children to do the same thing. You know, hockey won't last forever. But God will."

Suddenly a horrible noise came from the closed basement door behind us.

It was a strange noise, a cross between a crazed coyote and chalk scraping down the side of the chalkboard.

Pumpkin! He must have decided that spending the evening in the basement while we entertained company was a very uncool thing to do. And since he knew in his kitty heart that we would never have made him miss company on purpose, he took it upon himself to remind us where he was by howling and climbing up the wooden basement door at the same time.

The noise was loud enough to make the big hockey players sitting beside me go pale for an instant. Everyone's head jerked to the left, but no one said anything. Ryan Smith's eye twitched, and his nostrils flared, but he didn't ask the question: *What was that?*

Pumpkin made the sound again.

Have you ever been sound asleep at night, and then awakened by the sound of a tomcat howling outside your window? It's a horrible noise! They can sound a bit like a baby crying in the woods, or a woman screaming, and even now, when I know what it really is, shivers run up and down my back.

And I'm not scared easily.

Well, Pumpkin isn't exactly a tomcat anymore, but he can still make that weird sound. So as I watched the basement door

shiver and shake as Pumpkin banged against it, the strange crying wolf-cat sounds increased in volume.

Sid and the two Smith brothers looked at each other. They blinked and looked back at the door.

Jessica sighed and stood up.

"What *is* that?" Ryan Smith asked.

"It's just Pumpkin," Jessica said.

"A pumpkin?" the man exclaimed. You could see the look in everyone's eyes. *What kind of household tried to tell you that their vegetables scream and yell in the cellar below?*

"A very stupid Pumpkin," Jessica added. She opened the basement door.

Pumpkin slid down the wood door with a grunt, landing loudly on his feet, and then pattered across the kitchen floor.

He looked up at each of us carefully, his face arranged in a cat-like grin. Then, with a mighty bounce, he sprang up onto Ryan Smith's lap. There was a rip as Pumpkin's claw caught in the big man's pant leg.

I'll have to give Ryan Smith credit for being a brave man. He didn't flinch or toss Pumpkin aside. Instead, with a wide grin of his own, he began to stroke Pumpkin's back.

"Well," Ryan Smith said. "Another redhead, I see."

Pumpkin only purred louder.

* * *

When I went to bed that night I had an autographed hockey puck beside me on the bedside table. It read: *To Rusty Hill from Ryan Smith.*

"Just think of it as a late birthday present," Ryan had said as he slipped back into his winter coat. "And many thanks to you all for a delicious meal."

"He was perfect." I sighed as Dad admired the puck before turning out the bedroom light.

Dad smiled. "I'm glad you had a good evening, son."

"I'll never forget it," I said. "Ryan Smith came to our house! And he even liked our food!"

Dad sat down on the edge of the bed. "Rusty, I want you to remember one thing. God gave Ryan Smith some special talents. He can skate and play hockey better than the average person."

"You're telling me!"

"But Rusty, he's still just a person. No better, and no worse than many other people who don't happen to play professional hockey," Dad continued.

"I wish God would give me that talent," I

41

said. "I would love to be a hockey star. I'd love to be famous."

"God *has* given you talents," Dad began.

"I'm decent at hockey," I said modestly, "but I'm not *that* great."

"There are other talents," Dad said. "God picks the right talents for the right people. He has a special plan for each of us. We need to pray that God helps you and me—and Ryan Smith—to use our talents in the best way possible so that we can show others His love."

I really thought about that after Dad turned out the light.

I've always believed in God. God is important to me. But I wasn't sure just how important He was.

My brain wanted to say that God was more important than hockey.

But my heart wasn't so sure.

I fell asleep almost immediately, and I dreamed that I was playing hockey. There were all my favorite hockey stars, with Ryan Smith right in the middle of them all.

"Come play with us," Ryan called, beckoning with one hand.

I was skating like a superstar. I skated smoothly and handled the puck effortlessly, faking passes around all the professional players.

It would have been the best dream of my life.

Except for one little thing. I was just about to make another goal when a nagging feeling in the pit of my belly woke me up.

I had to go to the bathroom. *Again.*

This was going way too far. Something was wrong with me, and it was even interfering with my dreams.

4

I EMBARRASS
MYSELF AT HOCKEY

Rusty Hill!" Mrs. Rodney's voice was sharp. "I'm speaking to you."

I opened my eyes and looked around the classroom.

Opened my eyes? Had I actually fallen asleep during class? Mrs. Rodney wasn't going to be very happy. And if Mrs. Rodney was unhappy, then I was going to be unhappy too!

"Yes, Mrs. Rodney?" I asked innocently, being careful not to look my teacher in the eye.

Mrs. Rodney stared at me for a moment. "Do you think I'm stupid, boy?" she barked.

"Yes, Mrs. Rodney," I said, and then I flushed. "I mean no, Mrs. Rodney."

The teacher narrowed her eyes. "Were you sleeping?" she asked sharply.

I quickly shook my head.

"Then why were your eyes closed?" she asked.

I tried to think of a smart answer, but absolutely nothing came to mind. Why *had* my eyes been closed? I couldn't even remember dozing off. One moment I had been awake, struggling with my essay on outer space, and the next moment I had been asleep.

"I was just thinking," I finally said.

Mrs. Rodney took a deep breath and frowned. "Then think with your eyes open," she said.

"Yes, Mrs. Rodney," I said. I quickly began to write in my workbook. But the words swayed back and forth before my eyes, making me blink and squint in my effort to follow the sentences across the page.

I was confused. How could I have fallen asleep during class? What was wrong with me?

When school was dismissed, Brett walked beside me down the snowy sidewalk. He didn't seem to notice my confusion. "I read a joke about what to say if your boss catches you asleep at work," he said cheerfully.

"I wasn't asleep," I said.

"Yeah, right," Brett said. "You could have fooled me."

"All right," I said. "What *do* you say if your boss catches you asleep at work?"

"You should open your eyes, look upward, and say 'Amen!'" Brett laughed.

I thought about that for a moment, puzzled. "Amen?"

"What's wrong with you?" Brett asked. "Are you sleeping again?"

"I'm awake," I said. "But I just don't get it."

"This isn't rocket science," Brett said. "It's just a simple joke."

"Why would you say amen?"

"Because you want your boss to think you're praying, not asleep," Brett sighed. "Don't you get it?"

I shrugged my shoulders. "I wasn't at work," I said. "I was at school. And no one prays at school."

"It's just a joke, Rusty," Brett said. "I thought it was funny. But I guess I was wrong."

Now the snow-covered sidewalk in front of me seemed to sway back and forth, and my feet felt heavier and heavier with each step I took. I blinked my eyes and concentrated on walking straight.

"You're probably just tired," Brett said. "Up all night dreaming about Ryan Smith."

I *was* tired, but this seemed more than that.

Brett's voice seemed to trail away until it was nothing more than a hum in the background. I rubbed my forehead with one hand and took a deep breath of air.

I have to get home, I thought woodenly. I

felt like collapsing right there in the snow. Sleep. Wonderful sleep. I could sleep anywhere right now, even in the middle of the sidewalk. Even in a snowbank.

Brett watched as I struggled up my sidewalk.

"I'll see you at hockey practice," he called.

I didn't answer. It took all my strength to push the heavy outside door open. I stumbled inside, kicked my boots off, and headed straight for the couch. My eyes were closed before my head even hit the cushion.

It seemed only minutes later that someone was shaking my shoulders. "Rusty!" a voice called. I opened my eyes slowly.

"Hockey practice," Mom said.

I groaned and closed my eyes again.

"You've been sleeping for the last half hour," Mom said. "But you have to get up now. Hockey practice starts at 4:30."

A heavy weight seemed to press me firmly into the sofa cushion. *I'm sick,* I thought glumly. Really *sick. I mean, I'm so sick I can hardly move. It almost feels as if a 20-pound weight is sitting on my chest.*

A 20-pound weight? I opened my eyes.

Pumpkin smiled at me, and with a contented sigh shifted his weight slightly. No wonder I felt like an elephant was sitting on

me. One was! A big, happy, orange elephant.

I shoved Pumpkin off and looked around the room. Things still weren't right, even with the cat gone. The wall by the piano seemed crooked. I looked at it carefully. The wall seemed to lean at an impossible angle and, as I watched, the lights overhead wavered and then came on stronger than before.

"I'm not hungry," I said. "I'm sick." I blinked and spit a cat hair out of my mouth.

Mom passed me a piece of banana bread and a glass of milk. "Here," she said, "you'll feel better with something in your stomach."

Mom didn't seem to notice my dazed expression. When I thought about that later, I felt rather insulted! Do I go around looking dopey on a regular basis? Couldn't my own mother tell that something was wrong?

I ate the banana bread slowly. Within a few minutes I began to feel better. The living room wall straightened up by itself and the lights quit quivering overhead.

"Finish your milk," Mom ordered.

I drank it down in a couple of swallows and then followed Mom obediently out to the car. "Craig Michael Hill, where's your hockey bag?" Mom asked when I climbed into the front seat.

"In the house, I guess," I said. I climbed back out of the car and trotted inside. There

was a loud squawk as I stepped on Pumpkin's tail as I hurried down the hallway.

"Sorry," I called to the cat. But Pumpkin was gone, hiding someplace where clumsy boys couldn't step on him.

"It's OK if you stomp on me," I muttered, grabbing my hockey bag and pulling the door closed behind me. "But where's your Christian forgiveness when I step on you?"

We had driven only a few blocks when I suddenly remembered my skates. They were still in my bedroom, underneath my bed, where I had left them when I had replaced a broken lace.

Mom sighed loudly as she turned the vehicle around and headed back for home. "Rusty," she said, "I don't know what's wrong with you, but I hope this is just a stage. You just don't seem to be thinking straight these days!"

Here's another example of my stupidity. Why didn't I take that opportunity to tell Mom what had been happening lately? I should have been worried about all the strange things in my life. Wouldn't you think a person should be a wee bit concerned by their living room walls tipping sideways? Shouldn't you worry if you were falling asleep in the middle of class? And why was I going to the bathroom all the time?

Of course, now I know the answer to these questions. I should have told my mom what was going on. Maybe we could have prevented what happened next. But then again, maybe we couldn't have. I'm beginning to learn that God's plans for my life sometimes don't go the way I think they should. And that's a good thing, I guess, since we've already discovered that I'm not always the brightest person in the world!

But right then I had no idea what God had in store for me. I wasn't thinking straight. And it really wasn't my fault.

But we'll get to that soon enough.

Coach Wilson was in a bad mood. He barked out orders like a drill sergeant. "You guys have been playing like a bunch of girls lately," he said, glaring at all of us.

Our goalie was a girl, and she turned and frowned at the coach.

"Oh," Coach Wilson said, hesitating for a moment. "Sorry. Let me phrase that differently. You guys have been playing like a bunch of wimps," he continued, his voice rising. "And I'm tired of it. Now get out there and move!"

We did our stretches and warm-up exercises in front of Coach Wilson. At first I felt totally fine. I jumped and stretched and groaned

with the rest of the guys.

Then it began to happen again.

I had been watching Crystal, the goalie, as she did jumping jacks ahead of me. It was strange how girls had become less annoying lately. That didn't include Jessica, of course. She was a sister, and not a real girl. But other girls were suddenly interesting.

So as I exercised I watched Crystal out of the corner of my eye. At first everything looked normal. Crystal's blond hair bounced up and down with every jump. Then something weird began to happen. Crystal's hair began to sprout and grow. Soon it was mass of hair, a cloud of hair that billowed and swirled around her like a cape. I blinked and looked at Crystal again. She was gone.

Now two Coach Wilsons stood in front of me. I looked at the one on the left, and then the one on the right. Which one was the real coach? Why was his face so red? Why was he pointing at me?

"Hill!" Coach Wilson bellowed. "Get skating."

I looked around me.

I was standing alone in the middle of the ice. The rest of the team were skating laps around the arena, moving easily.

Brett waved at me. "Come on, Rusty," he called.

I stared at the team stupidly, and then looked down at my feet. *Where am I?*

"Move!" Coach Wilson roared.

My legs began to move on their own. I skated forward, and began my first lap. But as I skated something weird happened. A dark blur began on the outside of my vision. The blur narrowed and narrowed until soon I could see only a small circle straight in front of me.

I didn't know I was skating. I didn't know where I was. My brain was thick and fuzzy. *I'm playing pirates, Mommy,* I thought thickly.

When we were little, Jessica and I spent hours playing pirates under the kitchen table. We used an empty paper towel roll as our telescope, and we'd stare through the roll, looking for stormy weather and enemy ships.

Now all I could see was the small circle straight in front of me. *Pirates,* I thought. *Why am I skating if I'm a pirate? . . . Pumpkin? I'm sorry I stepped on your tail. Where's Pumpkin? . . . Where's Crystal? And Brett? And the pirates—*

The last thing I remember was the tunnel suddenly closing down.

There was a roar in my ears, and everything turned black.

And I didn't know where I was.

I didn't know anything at all.

HOSPITALS: WHAT
NO ONE TELLS YOU

The human brain is an amazing thing," a man's deep voice said. "Able to remember and sort information better than any computer. But look what happens when it's been injured."

A heavy weight seemed to be pressing against my chest. Again.

Pumpkin.

I blinked and opened my eyes.

Pumpkin wasn't there. Nothing was on my chest. And I had absolutely no idea where I was.

Maybe I was lying in the middle of the hockey rink.

Hockey rink? I looked around more carefully. The hockey rink was gone. I was in a strange bed. This wasn't my house. The walls were white and shiny, and I stared at them for a moment, trying to clear my thoughts.

The walls spun around me, turning to the

left for a moment, and then they straightened out. I closed my eyes.

Where am I? I said.

I don't think I said it out loud, because no one answered me. My parents were talking in great earnest to a tall man whom I had never seen before. The man was wearing a white lab coat. He had a stethoscope around his neck that he fidgeted with while talking to Mom and Dad.

He looked like a doctor.

I blinked again and thought, *He is a doctor.* And this white, white room . . . It was a hospital room.

I remembered falling during hockey practice. Maybe I'd broken something. I moved carefully on the bed. Something pulled on my right arm and I looked down at myself.

A piece of plastic tubing ran from a metal pole besides the bed into my arm. Tape held the tubing in place. It was an IV pole. I had an IV. I was in the hospital.

But I still couldn't understand why I was there. This time I spoke out loud. "What happened?" I asked.

"You collapsed on the ice because of a diabetic reaction," Dad said.

"A diabetic reaction?"

"You had a hyperglycemic reaction," the doctor said, "which means your blood sugar

level was very high." He shifted the stethoscope on his shoulder.

I stared at the doctor without saying anything. Blood sugar? Did a person actually have sugar in their blood? Nothing was making sense.

"Who are you?" I asked, looking at the man carefully.

"I'm Dr. Markowski," the man said, "and I've been taking care of you for the last day or so."

"Day or so?"

"This is Friday," Dad said.

"I had hockey practice on Thursday," I said. "Coach Wilson was yelling at me."

Dad nodded his head.

"Are you *sure* this is Friday?" I asked.

The doctor looked reassuringly at my parents. "Memory loss isn't that unusual," he said, "and it won't last."

"The last thing I remember was hockey practice on Thursday. Coach Wilson was yelling at me," I said again.

"I know," Dad said.

"We were playing pirates," I added. Then I stopped and thought for a moment. *Pirates? Where had that come from?*

"I've already told you this before," Dad said. He looked worried. "You were at hockey practice, and you passed out. You fell and hit

your head on the ice."

"I stepped on Pumpkin's tail," I said.

"No, you didn't," Mom said. "You were at hockey practice."

"At home," I said. "I stepped on Pumpkin's tail at home."

"Maybe you did," Mom said, "but you fell at hockey practice. You were unconscious."

"I hit my head and knocked myself out?"

Dr. Markowski looked at me. "You've got that in the wrong order. You passed out *first,*" he said, "and *then* you fell forward and gave your head a pretty good whack."

I reached up and rubbed the goose egg on my forehead. "Wasn't I wearing my helmet?" I asked.

Mom nodded her head. "You were."

"It's a good thing that you have a head like a rock," Dad said. He made a weak attempt to smile. "Otherwise you could have really hurt yourself!"

"Your helmet provided you a lot of protection," Dr. Markowski explained, "but your brain was shaken inside your skull, something like dropping a bowl of Jell-O."

"Jell-O?"

"Nothing may actually hit the Jell-O, but it gets shaken and scrambled," Dr. Markowski went on. "That's why you have a

concussion. We think the bump on your fore-head is from the face mask being pushed up and under the helmet."

"I have a concussion?" I asked.

"Yes," the doctor said. "And a lot more than that, Rusty. You have diabetes."

"Why am I so mixed up?" I asked. "Is it be-cause of my concussion?"

"Yes, a concussion can do that," Dr. Markowski continued. "Your blood sugars have obviously been high for some time now. That can also affect your thinking."

"How can Rusty have diabetes?" Mom asked. Her face looked pinched and worried. "No one in our family is a diabetic. And doesn't this mainly happen to old people?"

"There are two types of diabetes," the doc-tor said. "And yes, one type does tend to hap-pen to older people. But the type of diabetes Rusty has normally occurs in childhood. Recent studies seem to indicate that a virus of some sort can cause the disease in suscep-tible people."

"Rusty has been sick all month," Mom said. "We just thought he had caught the flu from Jessica."

Consider this my birthday present to you, dear brother.

"That may have been the start of it," Dr.

Markowski said, "but it's obviously become much more than just the flu."

"Are you saying that getting the flu can cause diabetes?" Dad asked.

Dr. Markowski shook his head. "Not for most people. But some viruses may trigger diabetes in susceptible people. And then again, it may have started for a totally different reason. We just don't know."

"When will I get better?" I asked. I propped myself up in bed, flinching as the IV in my arm pulled snugly.

"Rusty, you're past the crisis for now," Dr. Markowski said, "but diabetes doesn't go away. Once you have it, you have it forever. You'll have to stay in the hospital for a few days, maybe longer."

"Stay in the hospital!" I exclaimed. "I'm not sick!"

"You've been very sick," Mom said. "Don't you understand, Rusty? You have diabetes. And it's not going to go away."

"I'm not sick," I repeated stubbornly. And it was true. The room had quit spinning in the last few minutes, and my head seemed to be a bit clearer. The only problem was that I still felt very sleepy, but that would go away if I could just rest for a while.

How long wilt thou sleep, O sluggard? when

wilt thou arise out of thy sleep?

I scowled angrily. I didn't want to sleep. I wanted to go home, but everything was still fuzzy, and sleep seemed to be pulling at me from every direction like an eight-legged octopus tugging at its prey.

"You'll need your blood sugars monitored every few hours at first," the doctor said. "The nurses have been giving you insulin to treat your high blood sugars. I've ordered a bunch of blood work for you tomorrow, and you'll need to see a dietitian before you go home."

"I'd like to see the dietitian, too," Mom said.

"We recommend both parents attend with their child," Dr. Markowski said. "Diabetes is something that affects the entire family. It will be to Rusty's advantage if all of you become as knowledgeable about the disease as possible."

I flopped my head back on the bed.

"I still don't understand," I said. "I don't really even know what diabetes is."

"Your body isn't making insulin anymore," Dr. Markowski explained. "Without insulin you can't use sugar properly."

"What's insulin?" I said with a groan.

Dr. Markowski patted my shoulder. "Right now you're not well enough to really understand what's going on. Remember what I said

about the human brain being amazing? Well, your brain has been through quite a shock in the last few days. It was jostled when your head struck the ice. And the high blood sugar level in your body also affected your brain. That's why you passed out while you were skating. And that's why you were in a coma in the ambulance."

"In a coma?" I thought for a moment. There were pieces of Thursday evening caught in the far recesses of my memory. Coach Wilson leaning over me on the ice, his face as white as the skating rink ice. Whiter, even. Brett and Crystal and the other kids staring at me with wide eyes.

Being inside the ambulance. "You're going to be OK, Red," someone was saying. There was something strapped around my face, and I was struggling to pull it off.

"An oxygen mask," the voice continued.

I gave my head a shake, and the memories slid away.

"You gave your parents quite a scare," Dr. Markowski said.

"You can say that again," Mom said. "I thought you were going to die, Rusty."

"People *can* die," the doctor said. "A diabetic reaction is a very serious thing." He looked at me and sighed. "Rusty, I'll come back

tomorrow, and we'll talk more. Right now I don't think you're in the best condition for this discussion. I suspect that you're not going to remember much of what I've said today."

"Am I always going to have problems thinking?" I asked. I rubbed the goose egg on my head and wondered why I didn't feel more frightened. Everyone looked so worried, and the thought of my brain being injured should have scared me. But the problem seemed distant, unclear, as though it belonged to someone else. Anyone else but me.

Dr. Markowski smiled faintly. "No, Rusty," he said, "your brain isn't permanently injured. Soon you'll be back at school earning A's."

"That will be a first," I said.

A fool and his money are soon parted.

I frowned again. Where did *that* come from? Strange thoughts were shooting in and out of my head so fast that I could hardly think straight.

I yawned, and Dr. Markowski wished us all good luck. "I'll be back tomorrow morning to see you, Rusty," he promised. "I'm sure you'll be back to normal by then."

My parents looked at each other with anxious eyes once the doctor was gone

"I want to go home," I said.

"In a few days," Dad said. "First, the

nurses have to give you some special medicine to help you."

"I hate pills," I said.

"I don't know if it will be pills," Mom said slowly.

"Then what?"

Mom and Dad didn't answer. Instead they stared out the narrow hospital window. They didn't seem to know what to say.

I didn't either.

A wave of exhaustion rolled over me. With a sigh I closed my eyes and rolled onto my side.

I had something wrong with me. Diabetes. Whatever that was.

I was going to get some medicine to help me get better. Tomorrow I had to have some blood work done. I wished Dr. Markowski hadn't told me about that. I don't like needles that much.

To be perfectly honest, I *HATE* needles. I'd never admit it to my friends, but needles give me the creeps. They probably scare everyone else, too, but us tough guys just don't sit around and talk about it. I mean, what would we say? *I'm freaked out about being poked by the health nurse. Did you see how sharp that needle was? It was like a knife.*

That didn't sound very brave, and I've got an image to maintain. After all, the guys all

look up to Craig Michael Hill.

Last year in grade six I had gotten my hepatitis shot. That wouldn't have been too bad if the school hadn't sent home permission sheets for the shot in October, and we didn't get the shot until November! That means I had an entire month to worry and fret about the needle.

Of course, it hadn't been quite as bad as I had imagined.

In fact, it had been only mildly horrible. I hadn't screamed or passed out or anything like that.

So I'm still tough. That was good.

Now it sounded as though I'd be getting another needle tomorrow. *It's going to hurt.*

But right now I had something more important to worry about. Sleep. That's all I needed right now. Sleep. I couldn't worry about needles while I was asleep, could I?

The heavy weight began to press again on my chest. For once it felt good. It felt warm and safe and cozy.

Pumpkin. Curled up and keeping me safe.

The IV pole beside me buzzed softly. Somehow it seemed like Pumpkin's deep purr.

The last thing I remember was regretting that I had thrown Pumpkin down the basement steps. *Sorry, big guy,* I thought with a sigh. *I'll never do it again.*

6

THE STRANGE
MISS MCDONALD

A woman's voice called from somewhere far in the distance. I had been dreaming, and the voice seemed to creep right into my dreams.

"Come now, sweetie," the voice pleaded. "You really must wake up."

I moaned and rolled over in bed.

"Poor chap," the voice continued. "I really do hate to bother you, but you must get up."

My eyes twitched and thought about opening, then squeezed tightly together without me telling them to do so.

"Sweetie pie," the voice repeated.

The hospital! I remembered where I was before I even opened my eyes. I was in the hospital after falling at the hockey rink.

I threw the pillow off my head and sat up quickly.

I looked around the room in a daze.

My eyes came to focus on a large woman dressed in white. She stood beside my bed, a tender expression in her eyes. She looked sweetly—lovingly—at me, with the same expression on her face that Jessica had worn when looking at Ryan Smith.

I quickly glanced around the room to see who the woman was looking at.

It was a simple hospital room. The walls were painted a creamy white, and thick flowery curtains hung from the large window directly across from me. An empty hospital bed was against the far wall. The room was totally empty, except for me.

The nurse *was* smiling at me.

"Where are my parents?" I asked, turning again to face the beaming nurse.

"Now don't you worry about a thing," the woman said. "They just popped out for a wee moment, and I'm sure they'll be straight back. You were sleeping so soundly, you know." Her face radiated love, and I flinched without knowing why.

"Now, young man," the nurse said, "you must be very brave." She reached over and took my hand in her heavy warm hands.

I blushed in spite of myself and tried to politely pull my hand from her grip.

The woman didn't seem to notice. She

squeezed my hand tighter, patting it sweetly. "This won't be very nice," she continued. "If I'm brave—if *you're* brave—we can do it, I'm sure."

Do what?

"I'm hungry," I said.

"It will be suppertime in a wee moment," the nurse said. "You've been asleep since I came on at 3:00." Her palms were wet, and my hand slid in her grip as I tried to pull loose.

The woman grabbed my other hand and turned it over to look at my fingers. "Poor chap," the woman said. "I just hate to do this, but I must."

"Do what?" I felt my heart begin to pound in spite of the nurse's soft voice. She sighed deeply. "Why, I need to take your blood sugars, of course," she said.

"Take my what?" I asked blankly.

"Now don't try and stop me," the woman said. "I'll be as quick as a wink." She winked at me with a weak smile of her own and took hold of my second finger.

"What are you going to do?" I asked. My voice sounded a bit sharp even to myself.

The nurse didn't answer, but I fancied that her already pale and doughy face faded a shade paler. She washed my finger with a warm washcloth and then picked up a strange-looking object from a box on the bedside table.

"Just a tiny poke, dearie," she said. "Like a mosquito."

I thought her hand trembled, but maybe it was mine. All I can say is that someone trembled.

The woman touched the end of my finger with a strange pen-like object. I looked at the pen and narrowed my eyes. It wasn't a needle, but what was it? And blood sugars? How do you check your blood sugars? Obviously, you'd need some blood, and maybe—maybe—

"OUCH!" I suddenly yelled. Something sharp had darted into the end of my finger. Without thinking, I yanked my hand quite impolitely out of the nurse's grip and looked at the end of my finger. A perfect drop of bright-red blood was forming there. I stared in amazement as the drop bulged and then fell onto the blanket, leaving a small crimson circle.

"Oh, my!" the nurse exclaimed. "Quick! Quick!" She reached again for my finger and began to squeeze the end, milking another drop of blood out. "We mustn't waste your blood," she said. "You don't want me to have to poke you again, do you?"

Poke me AGAIN? Never! I held very still while the nurse squeezed my finger.

Another drop of blood slowly welled up. The woman's hand shook as she carefully drew the

blood into a tiny eyedropper, then used the eyedropper to work the blood onto a tab sticking out of a strange-looking machine.

"Oh, dear," she muttered. "I *do* hope we have enough blood."

"Enough blood?"

The machine began to blink.

The nurse sighed with relief. "Wonderful!" She turned to beam at me.

"What are you doing?" I asked, looking from the blinking machine to the end of my finger which was now beginning to throb.

"I am *so* sorry, young man," she apologized, putting extra emphasis on the word *so*. "It just breaks my heart to have to poke your finger like that. But we must do it, mustn't we?"

"Do what?" I asked.

"Why, check your blood sugars, of course."

I narrowed my eyes and looked more carefully at the nurse. Her name tag said she was Miss McDonald. She was older than I had thought nurses would be, with streaks of gray running through her tousled hair. Her motions were quick and birdlike. Even now she was fussing with my hand, wiping the last of the blood off my tender finger, and then swiping furtively at the soiled sheet, trying to get the traces of blood off the bedding.

"I just don't know *how* you're going to man-

age, young man," the nurse said. "Such a terrible, terrible thing for a young person to have to go through. My heart just breaks for you."

"That hurt," I said pitifully.

"Oh, I'm certain that it did," the nurse said, "but what can we do? Dr. Markowski has ordered that we have to take your blood sugars every four hours."

"Every four hours!"

"It's dreadful, just dreadful," Miss McDonald agreed. "And you're only 12 years old. I just don't know how you're going to manage."

"Manage what?"

"Well, of course you *will* manage," the woman went on. "You'll manage just fine, I'm certain. But it is such a difficult thing."

The machine let out a shrill beep. Miss McDonald stopped in mid-sentence and looked at the machine. "Wonderful!" she exclaimed.

"What?"

"Eight point four," she said. Her round face was now creased with a wide smile.

"What's eight four?" I asked.

"Why, your blood sugars, of course," the woman beamed. "I won't have to give you any insulin right now!"

"Insulin?"

"I was just dreading it," she said, "and I'm sure you were, too." With a final beaming smile

she picked up the machine and left the room.

When the nurse had gone I looked around the hospital room again. So white, so plain, so cold. Maybe this was just a strange dream. I had had a head injury, after all. Maybe I was just imagining the whole thing. The large nurse, the drops of blood . . . Why, they were only part of a very weird and wild dream.

I felt better for a moment.

Soon Miss McDonald was back with a tray of hospital food. She plunked it down loudly and lifted the lid on the largest plate. A hunk of unidentifiable meat looked up at me, surrounded by several cooked potatoes and a limp mass of something green.

"Asparagus," the nurse said, sniffing loudly. "Yummy. Asparagus is one of my favorite vegetables." She seemed satisfied with the meal and put the lid back on it. "It's very important that you eat every bite."

After Miss McDonald left the room I lifted the lid off the tray again. I was hungry, and my stomach growled at the smell of the food, but I wasn't too sure about the meal. I poked the lump of meat with the fork, trying to decide what it was. A cutlet of some sort, I guessed. But what type? Was it a pork chop?

I didn't like meat at the best of times. We ate very little meat in our family, mostly just

a bit now and then when we ate out at a restaurant. And I definitely didn't eat pork. I decided to leave this meat alone.

The potatoes weren't much better. They were already half cold and so hard that I had to lean firmly onto the fork before they'd consent to mashing. I looked all around the tray for some butter to put on the potatoes, but there was none to be found. The asparagus was even worse. I do eat asparagus, although it would never be considered one of my favorite vegetables. When Mom cooked asparagus it at least looked green when she was finished. These vegetable were limp, and a dirty brownish-green color. Like a cooked turtle, I decided, or something equally gross.

I sighed, and used my knife to hack a slimy bite off one asparagus stalk. I slowly popped the food into my mouth and chewed.

It wasn't very good.

In fact, it was awful.

I chewed the asparagus several times, finally crushing the pulp into an unappealing mass, and then swallowed. I took a bite or two of the dry potatoes before putting the lid back on the plate.

The glass of milk on the tray was still nice and cold, so I drank that all down quickly. And the small bowl of canned fruit also

looked quite tasty. Apricots. I've always loved canned fruit, and canned apricots are one of my favorites.

These weren't the same as my fruit at home, though. They were so hard my spoon couldn't cut them without slopping juice out of the bowl. I finally wiped my knife and fork off on the napkin, then used them to chop the apricots into bite-size pieces.

When I was finished, I looked around the room and sighed. I was still hungry. You probably know what they say about boys, how they never get filled up. "I think Rusty has a hollow leg," my mom had complained only last week. But there was no way I was going to eat anything else on that tray.

"I wonder what Jessica's eating right now," I said out loud. "You can be certain that it would be better than this."

I thought longingly of Mom's homemade lasagna. And a big green salad smothered in creamy salad dressing. Cottage cheese patties. Chocolate brownies with thick chocolate icing. Potato salad with little hunks of dill pickles chopped up into it. Homemade cinnamon buns with plump raisins toppling out of them. Or chocolate brownies—Oh, I said that one already.

You get the picture, I'm sure. The world is

full of delicious food, and I was stuck in the hospital eating this stuff!

"I'm not eating another bite of this junk," I muttered. "Even Pumpkin's canned cat food would look better."

I didn't say grace, I suddenly thought. *I didn't even think about it until now.*

"This meal wasn't worth praying for," I argued.

Every meal's worth praying for, my conscience argued back. *Some people don't have anything to eat at all.*

I had grown up saying grace at every meal. In fact, my parents like to tell the story of my meal at Mrs. Greenhorn's house when I was 2 years old. Mrs. Greenhorn was the older woman who had lived next door to our family for many years. Her face was as wrinkled as a prune, but her eyes were sharp and beady, following my every move. She'd invited my parents and Jessica and me over for dinner one day, and I had scolded her when she had started to eat before praying.

"You gotta thank Jesus," I had scolded, "or else He's going to get mad at you."

My parents had smoothed things over, and Mrs. Greenhorn remained a family friend until the day we moved away to my dad's next pastoring job.

But now my own childish voice seemed to pour into my head. *You gotta thank Jesus or else He's going to get mad at you.*

I don't suppose you're going to believe me, but I was actually scared.

I know, I know, I've told you what a tough guy I really am. But even tough guys get scared sometimes. Right now everything seemed to be going wrong. A strange nurse with a strange machine was poking drops of blood from my finger. She said she'd have to do it every four hours! I was alone and confused. And if I ever needed God, now was the time.

I sure wouldn't want to make God mad by forgetting to pray.

Sorry, God, I thought gloomily. *I'll try to do better. But sometimes it's hard.*

We had moved to Calgary two years before. Until then, I had always attended church school and was used to saying grace with my classmates before we ate.

It wasn't like that at public school, let me tell you. I had prayed secretly, silently, for the first few months of public school, hoping no one would notice when I looked down and closed my eyes.

Now I didn't even bother to do that.

We had talked about sinning recently at family worship. "God loves us even when we

do things wrong," my dad had explained.

"Then I guess I can go on sinning," I had said. Part of me was teasing, but another part of me was surprisingly serious.

My dad had answered with a memory verse, a short one, that I could still remember: "Blessed are they that hear the word of God and keep it."

I sighed and closed my eyes, leaning back into the bed.

I'm sorry, God, I really am, I prayed. *Please make me better so I can go home soon.*

I had diabetes, and that was all I knew. I sure hoped that they'd do something about it here at the hospital, and do something soon. Because if the poking me didn't kill me, the food certainly would!

Before long the heavy-set nurse was back again. She beamed at me, and then lifted the lid on my tray. The smile disappeared from her face. "Oh, my!" she scolded, "you didn't eat a thing."

"I had a few bites of potatoes," I said helpfully. "And a glass of milk."

"That's not good enough," Miss McDonald said. Frown lines gathered on her forehead. She took hold of the fork and knife and began to cut the meat into little pieces. "Here," she continued. "I want you to eat all of this."

I looked at the meat, and then back at the nurse. Was she kidding?

"Doesn't it smell yummy?" the woman asked. "Umm-ummm. Delicious." She smacked her lips.

"I don't eat meat," I said.

"Don't be silly," she said. "Everyone eats meat."

"My family doesn't."

"Well, I'm sorry, dear, but you're going to have to now," she said. "Diabetics need to monitor their protein intake. You've had insulin this morning, and you can't skip meals anymore."

She stabbed a piece of meat with the fork and lifted it to my mouth.

I pulled back in amazement and clamped my teeth together.

"Come on, sweetie," the nurse coaxed. "You need to eat some more."

"No!"

Miss McDonald's face fell. She looked so genuinely sad that for half a second I was tempted to open my mouth and eat the horrible-looking food. In fact, I started to open my mouth, and then I stopped.

"I'm sorry," I said, "but I just can't eat it."

Miss McDonald's face flushed. "Just one little bite?" she coaxed.

I shook my head again.

She held the fork up in front of my face and waved it around. "Open the door," she said, "and the train will go in."

"I'm not a garage," I said. "I'm sorry, but I can't eat any more."

Tears welled up in the nurse's eyes. Honest! I recognize tears when I see them. For a moment I was afraid that Miss McDonald would break down and cry. But she didn't. Instead she picked up the tray, gripping it so tightly that her knuckles turned white, and with one last pathetic look she left the room.

"You're going to be sick," she predicted as the door closed behind her. "Very, very sick."

Well, she was right. I did feel sick. But not because of the food.

I was in a strange bed in a strange room in a strange hospital with a VERY strange woman taking care of me. I had a disease that didn't make any sense to me. I'd been poked by a needle to have my blood checked for sugar, although I still didn't have a clue how anyone could have sugar in their blood.

If this was diabetes, I didn't want any part of it.

I wanted to go home, and I wanted to go home *now*.

God, I promise I won't fight with Jessica anymore. And I'll be nicer to Pumpkin, too.

There wasn't a heavy weight on my chest anymore.

But a big lump was stuck in my throat. And I didn't think it was my supper.

7

A TOUGH TRIP TO THE BATHROOM

I can't wait much longer," I moaned.

My bladder was pounding like an Indian war drum. *Boom, boom, boom, boom. Go-to-the-bath-room,* it cried.

I wanted to. But how was I supposed to get there?

I'd never been in a hospital before, unless you counted the time I was born. I couldn't remember that stay, of course, so I had no idea what a person was supposed to do when they were in the hospital.

The bathroom wasn't very far away. I could easily walk there, but what was I supposed to do with the IV apparatus that was connected to my arm?

I fidgeted and crossed my legs and looked at the call bell. I had been trying to decide whether I should ring for help, but I had fi-

nally decided against it. I didn't know how many nurses worked in the hospital, but with the way things had been going, I had a pretty good idea which nurse would answer the bell.

Miss McDonald.

I sat up and dangled my feet over the edge of the bed. Things were getting rather urgent now.

The IV pump was plugged into the wall beside the bed. I looked at the machine and thought carefully. I'm smart. Ingenious. If anyone could figure out how to get to the bathroom with an IV in their arm it would be me.

So think.

Obviously, the pump needed power to work. There were wheels on the pump, so it was made to be moved. But would the cord be long enough?

I stood up and cautiously rolled the IV pump forward. I was only a foot or so from the bathroom door when the IV jerked to a halt. I flinched as the tape pulled on my wrist and the needle shifted in my vein. I looked behind me and saw that the pump's extension cord was now stretched tight. That was as far as it was going to go.

Now I looked at the plastic tubing that connected me to the pump. It appeared to be about three feet long. Could I reach the toilet if I left the IV pump standing here?

Yes, I could, but just barely.

"This is crazy," I muttered to myself. "How am I supposed to get into the bathroom?"

My brains and athletic ability made it possible for me to slip inside the bathroom door. By stretching my right arm straight out toward the IV pole I was able to get up against the toilet.

"You'd think they'd have enough sense to make the extension cord a bit longer," I grumbled. "What happens to the people whose arms aren't as long as mine are?"

I wanted to shut the bathroom door, but there was no way that would be possible. And there was no way I was going to proceed if I couldn't shut the bathroom door. Someone could come into the room at any time. And Craig Michael Hill wasn't about to embarrass himself like that.

The situation was urgent. I cast one last frantic peek out the bathroom door. I hate to think that everyone in the world has to know what happened next, but you can probably guess who chose this time to enter the room.

"Hello there, sweetie pie," Miss McDonald called. "What are you doing?"

What was I doing!

I let out a girlie shriek and tried to twist sideways. The IV in my wrist twisted with me

like a snake, ripping at my skin and yanking me back into position.

"Don't be scared, young man," Miss McDonald soothed. "I've seen lots of people in such situations before."

"Well, you haven't seen me!" I screeched.

"I was just bringing you fresh towels," she went on, as though she hadn't heard a word I'd said, and walked toward the bathroom door as I desperately yanked my pajamas into the on position.

"I don't need towels!" I yelled frantically.

"Of course you do."

"SHUT THE BATHROOM DOOR!" I demanded.

Miss McDonald clucked to herself. "I would if I could," she said, "but you didn't bring the IV with you, and if I shut the door we'd pull the needle out. Besides"—and now she smiled sweetly—"I'll probably be poking you in the bum one of these days soon anyhow!"

My knee banged on the toilet, and the IV in my wrist pulled harder, running a sharp message to my brain: *Stand still NOW!*

"What do you mean, you'll be poking me, well, you know?" I asked, still not turning to face the woman.

"Why, buttocks are a perfect place to get insulin," the nurse said.

"WHAT?"

"Buttocks or your arms or your belly," Miss McDonald said calmly. She turned away from the door and flicked the blankets on the bed into place. When I was certain she wasn't looking at my direction anymore I carefully made my way through the door and angled toward my bed.

"There," the nurse said with satisfaction. "Isn't that tidier?"

I shrugged my shoulders. "Did you mean it?" I asked.

Miss McDonald looked a bit puzzled. "Well, yes," she said. "I do think the bed looks tidier now. Don't you?"

"No, not that," I said. "I mean, did you really mean you'd be poking me in my—in my—well, *there?*"

Miss McDonald nodded her head, setting her gray hair flapping. "I probably will," she said. "We have to keep rotating the sites where you get your shots."

"What shots?"

Now Miss McDonald sighed heavily. "Aren't you listening, young man? You have diabetes. We check your blood sugars, and that determines how much insulin you need. Then you get your insulin by a needle."

"A needle?"

"Right. And one of the places we can give you a shot is in your buttocks. But don't worry, dearie. As I said, I've given these shots to lots of people before."

I don't mind telling you that the thought of Miss McDonald giving yours truly a shot in that location was not a pretty thought. And while it's obvious that I'm about as tough a 12-year-old as you're going to find, even tough 12-year-olds have their breaking point.

This was mine.

I was going to break right here and right now. Or at the very least, find a way to *make* a break for it!

MY WEIRDO
ROOMMATE

I was sitting on the edge of the bed, planning how to tie the sheets together so I could climb out the second-story hospital window, when Mom and Dad walked into the room. I was so happy to see them I could have cried.

Well, not cried, maybe. I'm too old to cry. But I *was* glad to see them.

"You gotta get me outta here," I said. My voice cracked, but at that moment I didn't really care. I was cracking under this pressure, too. And someone had to rescue me.

Dad shook his head. His eyes looked sad.

"I'm serious, Dad," I insisted. "This place isn't a normal hospital; it's a nut house!"

"Rusty!"

"Honestly," I said. "The nurses are absolutely crazy. I've been poked by needles and had food shoved down my throat and someone

saw me standing by the toilet. Naked!"

Mom and Dad looked confused.

"She says she's going to poke me in the bare behind, Dad! What do you think of that?"

Mom tried to smile. "I don't think your behind is that big a deal to a nurse, Rusty," she said.

"It is to me!"

"Oh, come on, Rusty."

"All right!" My voice rose another octave. "If you don't think it's a big deal, then why don't you let the nurse poke *you* in—in—well, *there?* Here, push this bell and we'll call her. But you're going to be sorry."

Dad sighed. "Rusty, calm down," he said.

Calm down? I wasn't the type to get all excited about things, but this was more than a person could take. I think anyone would have been upset. Not just people who were scared of needles, either. (Not that I'm actually scared, maybe just a bit nervous.)

That's not the point. I had a good reason to be upset, don't you think?

Dad sat down on the edge of the bed, and looked at me seriously. For once I put my lips together and didn't say anything.

Obviously I wasn't going to be able to save myself. I mean, using the sheets as a rope probably wouldn't work very well—especially

with an IV hooked onto my arm! And I never would have been brave enough—I mean desperate enough—to pull that IV needle out.

"Rusty, I feel bad for you," Dad said slowly, "but there're some problems that even a dad can't solve."

"So what am I supposed to do?" I asked.

"Well, the first thing we need to do is pray about this," Dad said.

"I've already prayed!" I said. "I asked God to help me get out of the hospital. And I asked Him to take this stupid diabetes away."

Dad hesitated. "I'm not sure that's what we should be praying for."

"Well, of course it is!"

Dad groaned. "Rusty, I guess you're right. God *could* make your diabetes go away, but I don't think that's very likely to happen."

"Why not? God *can* do miracles, can't He? If He loves me, He should make me better."

"God is a lot smarter than we are," Dad said. "He doesn't cause sickness and suffering—that's Satan at work. But God is wise enough to use our problems to make something good out of them. God's plans aren't always the same as ours because He sees the big picture, not just the little spot that we're stuck in."

"Dad, being here in the hospital isn't just a

little spot," I said. "This is a *big problem.* And if God won't help me, who will?"

"Now you're making sense," Dad said.

I stopped for a moment. What had I said that made sense?

"You're right," Dad continued. "There isn't anyone but God who can help you. We need to pray that God's will be done in every part of our lives. That means we have to let Him decide how to make us healthy, and how to help us deal with things that scare us."

"You sound like a pastor," I said.

"I *am* a pastor," Dad said. This time he smiled a little.

Mom and Dad each took one of my hands, and after a moment we bowed our heads. For once I wasn't even worried that anyone would see my parents holding my hands. I was sick. And it felt good to have someone taking care of me.

Dad prayed for many things. He prayed that God would help me be healthy, and that the doctors and nurses would know how to best help me. He prayed that I would be brave and learn how to handle my diabetes. And then he prayed that we all would gain something from this bad experience.

We had just finished praying when the door to my room swung open. Two men dressed in

white walked into the room and looked around.

"That's the bed," one said, pointing at the empty bed across from me.

"Excuse us," the other man said. "We're just going to make a trade here, young man. We're going to take this empty bed, and give you one with a little more excitement."

The men grinned at each other.

"Hurry up!" a voice yelled from the hallway.

"His majesty beckons," the first man said.

The two men each took an end of the empty bed and rolled it out of the room.

"What do you think they're up to?" I hissed when everyone was out of sight.

Mom shrugged her shoulders. "I don't know," she said, "but I have a feeling we're about to find out."

"Idiots!" the voice called again from the hallway.

In a moment a different bed was slowly rolled through the doorway. A boy about my size lay on the bed with his leg raised in the air.

"Traction," Dad said softly.

The bed was the same as mine except for a huge metal frame that hung over the top of it. The boy's leg was pulled up in the air by a rope hooked to the top of the traction.

"Watch where you're going!" the kid groaned. "You drive worse than my mother!"

"Sorry," the man said. "We're just about there."

"You drive worse than my mother," the kid repeated. "An' she don't even have a driver's license!"

The men rolled the boy over to the empty space where the last bed had been.

"Not here," the boy complained.

The taller man frowned. "Where do you suggest we put you? In the bathroom? Or the closet?"

"I want to face the window," the kid said. "Turn me around."

"Then you won't be able to reach the call bell," the man replied.

"I don't need a call bell," the boy said. "I'll just yell. Now turn me around."

The men looked at each other and hesitated.

"Are you deaf?" the boy asked loudly. "Turn this bed around. *Now!*"

"Listen," the other man said. "Yelling isn't allowed in the hospital."

"So I won't yell," the kid said. He looked over at me. "I'll just get Rusty Red Head over there to ring the bell when I need something."

Oh, great. Wasn't it enough that I was stuck in the hospital with Miss McDonald and her needles? Now I had a roommate who was worse than Hayden Granger.

The men shrugged their shoulders and spun the bed around so the boy faced the window. "How's that?" they asked.

"That's better," the kid said. "Thanks."

"We're out of here," the men said. "Try to keep out of trouble, OK? Don't bug the nice nurses."

"How about stopping by the cafeteria and picking me up a hamburger?" the boy said. "That would make up for your lousy driving."

"Ha!" the men laughed. "Good luck, buddy." They started to leave the room.

"Jerks!"

One of the men stuck his head back into the room and smiled, showing a mouth of big white teeth. "And you have a nice day, too," he said with a grin.

I stared at the new boy. My mom and dad were staring, too.

He ignored us for a moment, gazing out the window with a serious look on his narrow face. Finally the boy turned and looked at us. "Hey there, Red Head," he said. "I'm Evan."

I didn't say anything at first. Maybe if I just ignored the kid he'd go away. It was pretty obvious that this guy wasn't going to be able to follow me around and bug me. Or beat me up. So it was safe to ignore him, if I could.

My mom elbowed me firmly in the ribs,

which made me decide that it would be polite for me to answer. So with a scowl at Mom I mumbled my name to the new kid.

"Can you ring the bell for me, Rusty?" Evan asked. "I haven't had anything to eat, and I'm starving."

"You don't want supper, trust me," I replied. "It was totally disgusting."

"Well, what do you think I should do?" Evan asked. "Starve to death?"

That was beginning to sound like an appropriate idea, but Mom glared at me again, so I decided to keep talking. "I can ring," I said, "but you're going to be sorry."

"H'mmm," Evan sighed. He looked around the room thoughtfully. "Well," he finally said, "maybe you could find a phone book and a phone. I think I'll order in something to eat."

"I doubt that they deliver to the hospital," Mom said, "unless you have a credit card, or some way of paying before they come."

"A credit card," Evan groaned. "Fat chance." The kid thought for a moment, then turned to face us. "Unless you'd let me use *your* credit card?"

I rolled my eyes at my parents and turned away. Evan was obviously going to be a pain in the neck.

"Hey, come look at this," the kid called. He

beckoned at me and my family.

"What?" I asked.

"My leg."

I hesitated. Why would I want to look at his leg?

"No, really. Come look," Evan said. "Today they drilled a great big screw right through my bone. It's kinda interesting."

They drilled a screw into his leg? Get real. More likely the kid had a screw loose in his head!

"I can't get up," I said. "Got my IV and all."

"Well, unplug it," Evan said.

I looked at my parents. My mom nodded her head.

"Can I unplug the IV?" I asked slowly.

"Well, of course you can," Mom said. "It has a battery on it, so it will work for quite a while when it's unplugged. How else would you get to the bathroom?"

Now that would have been useful to know earlier.

"You did unplug it when you went to the bathroom, didn't you?" Dad asked.

I felt my ears begin to flush. "Well, not exactly," I admitted.

"How did you get in there if you didn't unplug the IV?" Dad asked.

"With great difficulty. I'll tell you about it

later," I hissed, all too aware of Evan's full attention.

Dad looked over at the boy and smiled. "What happened to you?" he asked as he helped me unplug the IV.

"Broke my femur," Evan said. "Skateboarding."

"What's a femur?" Mom asked, looking interested.

"I dunno," the kid said. "The big bone in your leg, I guess."

I carefully pushed the IV across the room. "Skateboarding!" I exclaimed. "This is the middle of the winter!"

"Yeah," Evan said. "Guess it wasn't that smart a thing, huh? But it was sure a lot of fun while it lasted."

I stopped and stared with amazement at Evan's leg. It was bare and white, like a plucked chicken. But it was his knee that fascinated me. A huge, shiny, silver screw protruded through both sides of his knee and was wired up to the traction above his bed.

"Looks like a bolt off a car, doesn't it?" the boy said. He wiggled his toes slightly, and then flinched.

"How did they get the screw in your leg?" I asked in amazement.

"It wasn't so bad," Evan said. "They put me

out and everything, so I don't remember a thing. But the doc said they used a power drill to screw it in, something like the drill my old man has at home."

"That's gotta hurt," I said. "I mean, it's right through your knee."

"Yeah, but I'm tough," Evan said. "And it's not in my knee. It's in the bottom of my femur. That way they can pull my femur into the right position so it heals."

"Why didn't they just give you a cast?" I asked.

"Can't cast a broken femur," Evan said knowledgeably. "Won't heal that way."

"That's disgusting!" I backed up a step, still staring at the boy's leg.

"Rusty!" My mother frowned at me.

I didn't say anything, but I walked back to my bed and plugged the IV back in.

"How long will you be in traction?" Dad asked gently.

Evan shrugged. "I don't know," he said. "All Dr. Crest would tell me was that I'd be in traction for a long time. Whatever that means."

"That's all he'd say?" Mom asked.

"The guy's a real jerk," Evan said. "He said he'd talk to my parents. Fat chance."

No one said anything for a moment.

"My dad won't be coming in to see me,"

Evan volunteered. "He'll be glad to have me out of his hair, I can tell you."

"What about your mom?" Dad asked.

"She don't drive," Evan said. "So she won't be coming in, either."

"Oh," Dad said slowly. "You're going to be lonely."

Evan laughed. "Lonely?" he scoffed. "I doubt it. I'm glad to get rid of my family for a while."

"Really?"

"Really," Evan said. "But I sure could use Mom's credit card. How else can I pay for the food I need?"

"Well, now you have Rusty for company," Mom said.

I glared at her from my bed, but she ignored my look and smiled at Evan. "Is there anything we can get you? Maybe a magazine or something to help pass the time?"

"How about a hamburger?" Evan said quickly. "I'm starving. And I hear hospital food is awful."

"See?" I said to my parents. "I told you it was awful."

Dad laughed. "Hospital food is supposed to be awful," he said. "Otherwise you'd want to stay forever."

"Dad!"

"I'll tell you what," Dad said. "How would you like it if I popped down to the cafeteria and bought you two something to eat? Would you like to share a pizza?"

"Share a pizza?" Evan asked. "I could eat one on my own."

"I'll make it a large," Dad promised. "OK, Rusty?"

"I'll eat anything that doesn't eat me first!" I said quickly.

"And maybe a milkshake?" Evan looked hopeful. "I prefer strawberry."

"OK," Dad said. "Give me a few minutes. I'll be back quicker than you can say Chef Boyardee."

I smiled in spite of myself. "Dad, I don't think Chef Boyardee makes pizzas!"

"Well, then, how about I'll be back quicker than you can say McCain?"

"I'll be ready and waiting," I replied.

"Extra cheese," Evan called as the door shut behind Dad. "I like my pizzas real cheesy."

Evan and I had almost finished the large cheese pizza when the door swung open. In walked Miss McDonald with her equipment in one hand, and an enormous smile on her face.

"Time to check your blood sugars, darling," she sang out. Then she looked at the pizza and her eyes popped open wide. "Oh, no!" she ex-

claimed. "You can't eat that! Don't you know that diabetics have to follow a special diet? Where did this come from?"

DAD SAVES
THE DAY

The room was totally quiet for a moment. Then Evan let out a large belch and grinned at the nurse. "I know," he said brightly, "maybe the stork brought it."

Miss McDonald looked puzzled. "The stork?"

"This *is* a hospital, isn't it?" Evan said. "I've always been told that storks bring things to the hospital, such as babies."

The nurse's face dropped slightly. "Who are you?" she asked darkly. "Are you going to be my patient?"

"Evan Esposito at your service," the boy said calmly. "And who are you?"

"I'm Miss McDonald," the nurse said. A wrinkle appeared between her eyes.

"McDonald!" Evan said. "Perfect. I'll take a quarter pounder and a large order of fries."

The nurse's face flushed pink. "Oh, my," she said in alarm.

Dad interrupted the conversation. "Excuse me," he said, "but it wasn't a stork that brought the pizza—it was me. I didn't realize it would be a problem."

"Rusty will need to eat a special diet," Miss McDonald said. "Otherwise, we're going to have problems regulating his blood sugars."

Evan burped again, but no one looked at him. "Cool it, lady," he said, taking another chomp of the pizza. "If Rusty can't eat any more of it, I'll finish the rest."

The nurse looked at him, scowling.

Even shrugged and took another bite of pizza. "The milkshake wasn't that good, to tell the truth," he said. "They didn't use real fruit."

"I'm sorry," Dad told Miss McDonald, "but we know almost nothing about diabetes. I didn't get Rusty a milkshake because I realized that diabetics aren't supposed to have a lot of sugar. But it didn't occur to me that something like a pizza would cause a problem."

Miss McDonald spent a few minutes telling my parents about diets and medications and other boring stuff while I watched Evan lick the bottom of the pizza dish. Finally a call bell rang in the distance.

"I have to go," Miss McDonald said. She hurried out of the room.

"Miss McDonald," Evan said with a sneer. "Now there's a real Big Mac!" He threw his empty milkshake cup toward the garbage, but missed his target. The cup fell on the floor, splattering drops of pink milkshake on the linoleum. "Of course, I always did hate McDonalds," he said with a big yawn.

I wiped my face on the napkin and looked at Mom. "That was a great pizza," I said. "And I'm glad I ate a lot before the food police came barging into our room."

"I hope it won't cause you any problems," Mom said.

I shrugged. "I don't get it," I said. "How can something like pizza be bad for me?"

"That's what we're going to have to find out," Mom said.

Before long Miss McDonald came back and poked my finger with the little blood sugar poker. This time it hurt worse than ever, and it took every bit of my courage to keep from yelling.

And then I got a shot of insulin in my upper arm.

"I haven't given very many shots before," the nurse said apologetically, looking from me to my family. "I'm a new nurse, you

know, so I hope it didn't hurt too badly."

It had.

When Mom and Dad went home that evening I lay in the dark hospital room and stared up at the ceiling. Someone of lesser character and courage than I would have cried. But I didn't. No sir-ee. Craig Michael Hill never cries.

Unfortunately, I seemed to be coming down with a bad cold. My nose ran and my eyes burned and I couldn't help but sniff and snort a little in bed.

Evan was snoring while I sobbed, uh, I mean, I sniffed. He never heard a thing. But when I woke up a few hours later, I heard something strange. I would have sworn that Evan was crying in the bed across from me.

Of course, it couldn't have been crying. Kids like Evan never cry. They go through life stealing little kids' lunch money. They make teachers take extra long mental stress breaks, and they don't ever go to church.

That kind of kid never cries.

No, God didn't need to worry about kids like Evan. They could take care of themselves.

10

ME AND THE POKEY PEN

I woke up early the next morning. Evan was snoring again, but the sounds of the hospital still drifted through the door. Something heavy and metal rolled by in the hallway, a cart of some sort, I imagined. A baby wailed loudly, and someone with hard-soled shoes clip-clopped past the door. A voice called, and there was laughter farther away down the hallway.

What could anyone laugh at in a hospital?

I stared at the ceiling and frowned. My watch said it was 7:00. Before long someone would come into my room and poke my finger again. They'd come back and stick a needle in my arm or my behind. I'd have a breakfast of some sort, and then I'd have to wait until later for the whole procedure to happen again.

I couldn't stay in the bed any longer. With

a sigh I swung my feet over the edge of the bed and unplugged the IV pole. Holding the cold metal in my right hand, I wheeled the pole into the bathroom and shut the door firmly behind myself.

As I washed my hands at the sink, I looked at my reflection in the mirror. I didn't look any different than usual. There was my flame-red hair, standing on end as if I'd just seen a ghost. My freckles, my square chin, my dimple that I didn't want anyone to notice—they all stared back at me.

I wet my hair with the comb and tried to make myself look neater, but it was a wasted effort. My hair seemed to repel the water and bounced straight back into its wild pose. I sighed and pulled the collar of my pajamas into place.

How could I look the same? My life was so different now.

It was hard to believe that only a few days ago I was on top of the world. Ryan Smith had had supper at my house.

It didn't seem very important anymore.

I guess I was feeling pretty sorry for myself, because without even realizing it, tears started to trickle down the side of my face. I wiped them away angrily and splashed cold water on my cheeks.

What am I crying for? I wondered. *I'm too tough to cry.*

You're crying because you're scared, I answered myself almost immediately.

Scared.

Of a little needle.

I put the toilet lid down and sat on top of it, thinking for a moment.

There's absolutely nothing to be scared of, I told myself firmly. *They use a very small needle. I can hardly feel a thing. Just don't think about it, and everything will be OK.*

I closed my eyes.

Dear Jesus, I prayed, *You know that I'm not the best person at praying. I hope You'll still take the time to listen to me. Please help me. I want my diabetes to go away. Will You do that for me? I'd love You a lot if You'd just make me well again.*

I wondered if God could hear me. Does God come into hospital bathrooms and listen to kids who sit on top of the toilet and pray?

Lo, I am with you alway, even until the end of the world.

There. I must know more memory verses than I had realized, because that one popped into my head all by itself.

God was with me always, even until the end of the world. Did that mean that He was

there in the hospital bathroom? I smiled in spite of myself and stood up again. I blew my nose on a piece of toilet paper and unlocked the door.

God could make me better. He could do anything He wanted to do. I just needed to find some way to persuade God to do what *I* wanted. What *I* needed.

Today I'd pray a hundred times an hour. I'd ask God to fix me and get me home safely. And maybe, just maybe, if I prayed long and hard enough, God would see things my way.

Evan was awake when I got back into the room. He didn't look very cheerful, and there were dark circles under his eyes. He didn't look like he'd slept very well.

"Ring the bell, Rusty Red Head," he ordered as soon as he saw me.

"What do you need?" I asked, stretching. "Maybe I can get it for you."

"Just ring the bell," the boy ordered.

I pushed the call bell slowly. *Please don't let it be Miss McDonald,* I thought earnestly. *Anyone but her.*

My prayers were answered when a long-haired nurse in a bright-blue uniform pushed our door open.

"Can I help you boys?" she asked cheerfully, looking around the room.

"Evan needs something," I said, pointing to the frowning boy in traction.

The nurse smiled at me, and I noticed how pretty she was—and how different she looked from Miss McDonald. Her eyes were as blue as her uniform, and she had a dimple in her pink cheek that looked 100 percent better than my dimple ever did. Her hair tumbled down to her shoulders like a silken curtain, and she even smelled good—like a flower, maybe, or a piece of sweet fruit.

I was beginning to think that today had definite possibilities. I mean, if someone had to come into my room and poke my finger with a needle, this would be who I'd choose to do it.

Evan didn't look nearly as happy to see the pretty nurse as I was. In fact, he looked her up and down, and his frown deepened.

"Hi," the nurse said, flashing me her dimple again. "I'm Shelly, and I'm the lucky one who was assigned to your room today."

"Come here!" Evan ordered.

"Sure," Shelly said. She walked over to the bed and looked down at Evan. "What do you need?"

"This tube," Evan said. Then he glanced at me and lowered his voice.

I listened with interest.

"Your tube?" she asked.

107

Evan looked sideways toward me and narrowed his eyes. "Can't you take the awful thing out?" he hissed.

I couldn't see what Evan was talking about. There was no IV by his bed—no tubes connected anywhere that I could see.

But the nurse seemed to know what he was talking about. She nodded her head and glanced over at me. "Are you sure you feel well enough?" Shelly asked quietly. "Once the tube is gone you're going to have to move a bit more in bed."

"Listen, honey," Evan said, "I'll be fine. Just take it out."

"OK." Shelly pulled the curtain around Evan's bed briskly. "I'll be back in a few minutes with my equipment."

I propped myself up on the pillow, preparing to watch the activities across the room. Hey, I was bored. There was no TV, nothing going on, and the mystery of Evan and his tube was better than nothing.

Shelly came back in a minute or two with a handful of supplies. She disappeared behind the curtain, so all I could see was the bottom of her blue uniform and her white shoes as she walked around the bed. She and Evan talked in low voices for a minute.

"Do you have to look?" Evan once asked sharply.

Shelly said something in a soothing voice.

"Well, hurry up," Evan said.

In a minute she pulled Evan's curtain open, and then left with her supplies in one hand. "I'll be back to check your blood sugars," she said as she walked past my bed. "And, hopefully, we can remove your IV this morning so that you can start moving around a bit easier, OK?"

I nodded my head. My fingers began to tingle just thinking about the needle, and I looked down at them. I have long fingers for a boy—my dad said I'd be a good piano player "if you'd only practice now and then!" My nails were too short because I chewed them, but that didn't bother me right now. What did bother me was the small tender spots on the end of most of my fingers, spots where I'd already been poked for a drop of blood for the blood sugar machine.

A vampire bat, I thought gloomily. The machine was like a hungry, blood-sucking vampire bat, biting my finger and sucking out one drop of blood at a time. And I didn't like it one bit.

Evan interrupted my thoughts once again. "Will you ring the bell, Rusty?" he asked. "I really gotta go."

"Well, go!" I said with a sigh, still studying my fingers carefully.

"Come on," Evan said. "How do you think I'm going to get to the bathroom? Fly, maybe? Or crawl on my back with my leg in the air?"

I thought about that for a moment. "That's a good question. How *are* you going to go to the bathroom?"

"Mind your own business," Evan said shortly. "Just ring the bell like I asked."

I pushed the bell, and Shelly came into our room almost immediately. She was carrying the dreaded blood sugar machine with her, and my fingers tucked themselves under my covers without my telling them to move.

"Evan needs you again," I said.

She glanced over at Evan.

"I gotta go," Evan said. "And quick."

Shelly smiled. "Well, of course you do," she said. "I should have thought about that, shouldn't I? Just stay put for a moment, OK?"

She put the blood sugar machine down and quickly left the room.

I watched the blood sugar machine out of the corner of my eye as we waited for Shelly's return. *I should hide the thing,* I thought, but hiding the machine wouldn't solve the problem, now would it?

God, it's me, Rusty, again. Please; You gotta help me. Make my diabetes go away. Please, make my diabetes go away. And maybe while

You're at it, You can make Evan go away, too, because he's almost as bad as a needle!

Even as I prayed, doubts sprang into my mind like water rushing down the drain. Dr. Markowski had said that once you get diabetes, you have it forever. Could God actually make me better? WOULD God actually make me better?

I shouldn't doubt, I thought quickly. *I need to have faith. God can do anything, can't He?*

Yes, He can! But I needed to ask Him the right way. But what exactly was the right way to get God to make me healthy again? I wasn't sure.

Shelly came back into the room and passed Evan a shiny silver bottle. She smiled at the boy, then pulled the curtains around his bed. I wondered why he hadn't had to use the bottle yesterday, and then I put two and two together. Shelly had taken out a tube. Now I knew what kind of tube Evan had. Yuck!

Suddenly having my finger poked didn't seem too bad. At least I could get up and move around and do all the things that a person takes for granted in their normal living. Poor Evan was really stuck!

Shelly picked up the blood sugar machine and set it on the bedside table. "What do you

think your blood sugar will be this morning?" she asked.

I shrugged my shoulders. "I dunno."

"What was it yesterday?"

I shrugged again. "I have no idea. Am I supposed to keep track of them?"

Shelly wrinkled her forehead. "Well," she said, "the nurses keep track of your blood sugars on your chart, but you should, too. When you go home you're going to want to know how to tell if your blood sugars are too high, or too low."

"Am I going to have my blood sugars checked at home, too?" I asked. My fingers buried themselves a bit deeper under the covers.

"Of course you are," Shelly said brightly. "At least three or four times a day."

"Who's going to do it?" I asked.

"Why, you are!" Shelly said.

"Me?"

Shelly nodded her head. "Sure," she said. "You're 12 years old, aren't you?"

"I turned 12 just a little while ago," I said nervously. "And I know that there's no way I can poke myself with that thing."

"Sure you can!" Shelly said. "And soon you'll be giving yourself insulin, too."

"Insulin!" I croaked. "There's no way I'll be poking myself in the behind!"

"Most diabetics give themselves insulin in their stomach," Shelly said with a faint smile. "But we won't worry about that today. Let's just concentrate on taking your blood sugars."

She went to the sink and wet a washcloth, then passed it to me. "First, you need to decide which finger you want to poke and wash it so that you don't get any germs in your puncture."

My hands were like nervous mice hiding in a mouse hole with Pumpkin standing at the door, and I had to force them out from under the covers. I looked at each finger carefully, trying to decide which one I was going to sacrifice today.

"Just pick one," Shelly said with a grin. "We haven't got all day."

I finally held out the small finger on my left hand.

"OK," Shelly said. "Now give it a wipe."

I polished my finger until it was so clean it sparkled, and I would have kept washing it if Shelly hadn't finally taken the washcloth away with a sigh. "Now hold the pen up to your finger, push here . . . and *pop,* it gives you a little poke. Here, try it." She passed me the pen.

I held the end of the pen gingerly, as though it was a balloon at a birthday party. Remember the birthday party game that some kids play in which you tie a balloon around

your ankle, and then try to stomp on everyone else's balloon while keeping your own balloon safe? I played that game at my tenth birthday party, and I hated it. Especially since Hayden Granger went around stomping on kids' feet as often as he stomped on their balloons. Pumpkin hated the game, too. He ran downstairs and hid when the first balloon exploded.

That's exactly how I felt with the pokey pen in my hands.

"It's not going to attack you," Shelly said, reading my thoughts. "Here, now," she continued. "Do this. Hold the end of the pen to your clean finger, and then push the button here."

I looked at my little finger. My little finger stared back at the pen and considered climbing back under the covers.

Just then Evan yelled from behind the curtain. "I'm finished."

It made me jump, and I almost dropped the pen.

"Just a moment," Shelly said soothingly. "I'm helping Rusty now."

"I'm gonna spill the bottle," Evan threatened.

"I can wait," I said quickly, putting the pen down on the bedside table. "You'd better make sure Evan's OK."

"Oh, such a caring young man!" Shelly

smiled, showing her dimple again, and then slipped over to Evan's bed.

She was back much too quickly and, after washing her hands, forced the pen back into my stiff fingers. "OK, buster, it's simple. Put the pen against your finger and push the button."

I took a deep breath and slowly moved the pen toward my finger. When it touched the tip, I jumped.

"Not there," Shelly instructed. "You don't want to poke the very end of your finger—there are too many nerves there. Position the pen off to the side a bit."

I shifted the pen over.

"Perfect!" Shelly beamed. "Now push the button."

I tried. I really did. But my brain was on the same side as the rest of my body. We're a team, my brain and me. And there was no way that my brain was going to make my fingers do anything to hurt the rest of us.

I couldn't push the button. And I really tried.

Shelly studied my face carefully. With an encouraging smile, she took the pen and gave the end a flick. The needle snapped out and poked my finger. A round drop of bright-red blood welled up. As I watched, Shelly moved the blood over to the tab on the blood sugar

machine. The lights blinked, and in a moment the number 3.4 flashed on the screen in bright-green letters.

"You're a bit low," Shelly said. "I'm going to bring your breakfast right away, then we'll check it later."

"What's it supposed to be?" I asked, wiping the end of my finger with a tissue.

"Your blood sugars should be between four and eight," Shelly explained, "give or take a bit, I suppose." She stood up and smiled at me. "You did very well," she said.

I flushed a bit, feeling my ears turn red. "I didn't do a thing," I said.

"That's for sure," Evan called. "What a chicken!"

"You almost did it," Shelly said, ignoring Evan. "Don't worry, Rusty, it will happen. Every time you try, you get one step closer to succeeding. Now, I'm going to go and grab the breakfast trays for you two."

As soon as Shelly left the room Evan propped himself up on one elbow and stared across at me. "Way to go, tough guy!" Evan called. "What's the matter with you? Can't stand a little poke in the finger?"

I'd like to give you a little poke in the nose, I thought to myself. Wisely, I kept my thoughts to myself and didn't answer.

I didn't even pay attention to Evan when he began to grumble about the food. "No Frosted Flakes," he complained. "And the toast is cold."

"It's fine," I said, taking a bite. At least it had butter.

"Ring the bell, Rusty," Evan said. "I need some strawberry jam."

I sighed and rang the bell. Cold toast didn't matter to me. But poking myself with that horrible machine did. *God, where are You? I don't think I can do this, even with someone as nice as Shelly helping me. You were supposed to help me, remember? I don't want diabetes anymore. I just want to go home, and get back to being a normal kid.*

11

THE EVIL SISTER COMES TO VISIT

The next night was just as awful as the first one had been. I slept poorly, tossing and turning and thinking about that awful poky pen. I had tried to check my blood sugars all day, and I hadn't succeeded even once. Shelly had removed the IV, and that had hurt, too. I sighed and rubbed my arm where the hair had been yanked out by the IV tape.

The room was pitch-black, and I wondered why I was awake. Had I heard something?

Then I heard it again.

"Watch out!" Evan said in a loud voice.

I looked around the room. Who was Evan talking to?

He was quiet for a moment, and then he laughed. "No," he said. "That didn't hurt." There was another pause, and his voice grew louder again. "Watch out!"

"Psstt," I hissed. "Evan, what's wrong?"

He didn't answer.

He's talking in his sleep, I finally decided.

The room was quiet for a few moments, and I closed my eyes. I was just beginning to drift back to sleep when Evan began to yell.

"No! No! No!" he hollered.

"Would you be still?" I yelled back.

"You shut up," Evan replied.

I reached over and turned the light on by my bed. Evan was lying on his bed, his eyes closed. As I watched, he twitched and moved his mouth, and then lay quietly again.

"Now I've seen everything," I muttered, flipping the light off again. "It's not enough that he talks in his sleep, he also argues."

The room remained quiet, then a baby began to cry down the hallway, and the voice of a woman in the distance drifted through the door. I tried to get back to sleep without success.

Great. Just great. It's bad enough that I have to sleep at the hospital. It's even worse that I have to lie in bed wide awake.

Finally I gave up trying to sleep. Maybe I could use this time to pray.

I think I prayed quite well. I told God in specific detail what He could do to make my life better. First, He could make my diabetes go away. Next, He could get me out of this

119

hospital and back to my house.

I could manage Jessica on my own. Pumpkin was welcome to sit on my chest and shed hair on my face. But I didn't want to be sick anymore.

I know that I was being selfish. I'm not normally a selfish person. Honest. But being sick is a tough thing for anyone.

Finally, at 8:00, I climbed out of bed and dressed in my regular clothes.

Evan watched me from across the room. "Where're ya going?" he asked as I pulled my shoes on.

"For a walk," I answered briefly.

"Take me with you," he said.

I looked at the boy, and then at the enormous hospital bed. "You gotta be kidding," I said incredulously. "What am I supposed to do—carry you?"

"Push the bed, dummy!" Evan said. "It does have wheels, you know."

"I'm not pushing your bed around the hospital."

"Ah, come on," Evan coaxed. "I saw you praying last night, so you must be a Christian. Doesn't that mean you hafta be nice to me?"

"Nope."

"Have a heart," Evan said. "You don't plan on leaving me here to rot in this bed for the

next month or so, do you?"

"I'm not pushing you around on that bed," I said. And I slipped out of the room before I could hear what Evan had to say next.

I walked up and down the long corridor for 15 minutes or so. Before long an enormous cart full of meal trays was rolled down the hallway.

Shelly came out of a small room, surrounded by a group of nurses. She saw me in the hall and waved.

"I'm coming to see you again," she called cheerfully. "Today's the day, Rusty."

When she came in, I tried, but I still couldn't take my blood sugars. And I closed my eyes when Shelly gave me my insulin needle in the belly.

"That seems like a weird place to get a shot," I finally said when she was finished.

"Actually, it's the perfect place for insulin," Shelly said. "Easy to reach, and since your belly doesn't move as much as your arms and legs do, it doesn't cause much discomfort."

Yeah, right.

"Face it, Shelly," Evan called from his bed, "the guy's a big chicken. A Chicken McNugget. And he ain't about to give himself a poke."

I figured Evan was probably right for once.

Mom and Dad came to the hospital around

10:00, and we went to an incredibly boring lecture on diabetes and a proper diet.

Mom and Dad both had notepads and pens, and they both scribbled constantly, writing down pages of instructions and suggestions. Dad embarrassed me by asking several questions, and I kept sinking down lower and lower in my chair.

God, if You love me You'll make my diabetes go away. Then I won't need to listen to this garbage about eating.

Almost everyone at the lecture was old enough to be my grandparents. One girl across the room caught my attention, though, and I spent some time watching her blow enormous bubbles with some pink gum. She had long hair dyed in a strange bright-pink color (almost matching her gum), and her tongue was pierced. Both things amazed me. Why would anyone want to make their hair a weird color? I'd be happy to be a plain brunette or blond instead of being a redhead. And having your tongue pierced had to hurt. I couldn't stand a little poke in my finger, not to mention a big needle in the tongue! (Plus I wondered how she made bubbles with a stud stuck through her tongue. Didn't it hurt?)

I moved my tongue inside my mouth, thinking about the process that one went

through to shape the gum and then blow it into a bubble.

Dad elbowed me in the side once. "Pay attention," he said.

I nodded my head and slumped lower in the chair. *Anytime now, God. Please get rid of my diabetes. Forever.*

* * *

I got back into my room just before dinner arrived.

"That was very informative," Mom said, sinking down in the chair by my bed. "I really learned a lot."

"That was boring," I said.

Dad nodded. "Yeah, it was. But I'm still glad I came. You know, I don't think it's going to be that difficult following a diabetic diet. It's basically just a good, healthy way of eating without too much sugar or fat."

"That's easy for you to say," I snapped. "You don't have to eat like a diabetic."

"Oh, but I will," Dad said.

"Give your head a shake, Dad," I said, looking at both my parents. "No one would give up sugar without a good reason."

Mom smiled. "Rusty, I expect that we'll all start eating a bit differently at home. None of us really need sugar or greasy foods."

"Jessica would die before she gave up chocolate," I said. That thought made me smile briefly.

"That reminds me, Rusty," Mom said. "Jessica's going to be here in a few minutes to see you."

"To see me?"

Mom nodded her head. "She gets out of school early today—teacher prep day, or something like that. Her friend Meagan agreed to drop her off at the hospital."

I groaned. "Can't I even be sick in peace?"

"Jessica's been worried about you," Dad said with a laugh. "Believe it or not."

"I doubt it," I said. "She must enjoy having the bathroom to herself."

"True enough," Mom agreed, "but she's still missed you."

I wasn't convinced. Jessica would miss me about as much as a dog missed his fleas.

Shelly popped into the room and set a tray of food down on Evan's table. "Here you go," she said brightly. Then she disappeared, only to return in a moment with a tray for me. "A meal fit for a king," she said with a smirk.

I rolled my eyes.

"Here, King," she laughed. "Here, King!"

"That's about it," I groaned. "Dog food!" I knew I'd been thinking about dogs for a reason.

"Don't eat for a moment, OK?" Shelly said. "I want to check your blood sugars before you start."

"Let's do it quick," I said. My heart began to pound louder than ever.

"Quick?" Shelly said. "That's a change from your normal attitude."

I know something you don't know, I thought gloomily. *My sister's coming any minute now, and the last thing I need is to give her something else to laugh at.*

Shelly briskly set the glucometer and other equipment up on the bedside table. "OK, Rusty," Shelly said, passing me a washcloth. "This time you're going to do it yourself."

"Please," I begged. "Not today. Just poke me quick so I can get it over with."

"Rusty," Dad said. He raised his eyebrows and looked at me, and then back to the blood sugar equipment.

"I can't do it, Dad," I said. "I've tried, but I can't do it."

Evan began to cluck like a chicken from across the room, and it took all my control to not throw my plate at him.

"Well, you start," Shelly said. "Do as much as you can, and I'll finish the rest for you."

With a frown, I grabbed the warm washcloth and wiped my finger quickly.

"Tell your parents what you're doing," Shelly instructed.

"I'm washing my finger," I snapped.

Shelly gazed at me steadily, and I felt myself begin to flush. "Sorry," I mumbled.

"I would think so," Dad said. "Now, keep going."

"I'm washing my finger so I don't get germs when I poke myself," I said. I looked at the instruments on the bedside table and finally picked up the poky pen. "You put this on your finger—not at the very end, or it will hurt too much," I continued. "And then you push the button. A needle flicks out and pricks your finger."

"Let's see you do it," Mom said. She leaned forward, watching with interest.

My fingers began to twitch, but I forced them to remain on top of the covers. My eyes flicked around the room, coming to rest on Evan, who had quit clucking and was smirking at me from his bed.

Mom and Dad were also staring at my every move, spellbound as though I was a magician about to pull a rabbit out of a hat. I'd do a trick if I were a magician: I'd disappear into thin air. No more blood sugars. No more insulin. Nothing but peace and quiet and a game of hockey to play now and then.

But I wasn't a magician.

So I placed the end of the pen to my finger and shifted things slightly. My other hand clutched the pen tightly, and my thumb shifted nervously above the switch. When everything was in position, I hesitated. *I'll count to three,* I told myself. *And at three, I'll push the button.*

Shelly nodded her head and smiled at me. I looked away quickly.

One, two—

The door burst open with a bang, and Jessica bounded through the door. "Well," she exclaimed. "I finally found you, little brother." She tossed her head, setting her auburn curls off in a wave of color, and dropped her heavy backpack down on the floor with a thud. "Do you know how big this hospital is?"

"Oh-la-la!" Evan whistled from across the room.

Jessica ignored the boy, and bounced across the room toward my bed. "Hi, redhead!" she said. "Whatcha doing?"

I rolled my eyes and shifted the pen to my other hand. "What does it look like?" I growled. "I'm about to perform surgery."

"Hopefully, it's a lobotomy," Jessica said with a grin.

"What?"

"A lobotomy," Jessica teased. "You know,

brain surgery. Heaven knows you need it."

"Jessica!" Dad said. He glared at the girl for a moment. "Why don't we try to avoid a fight for a couple minutes?"

"We're not fighting," Jessica said. She reached over and grabbed me by the ears and planted a kiss on the top of my head. "I'm just trying to show my baby brother that I love him."

"A little less love would be good," I said with a frown, swiping at the top of my head.

Mom groaned. "Just poke yourself, Rusty, and get it over with. We don't have all day."

"I'm not poking myself with Jessica watching," I said, setting the pen down on the bed. "And that's final."

Shelly sighed. "I don't mean to rush you," she said, looking at me, "but I have a lot of other patients to take care of, too. Maybe I *should* just poke you, and get on to other things."

"I think you're right," I agreed. I held out the finger that I had cleaned recently. "Here you go."

"I'll poke Rusty," Jessica offered. Her blue eyes were twinkling, and the dimple in her chin appeared.

"No way!" I said, pulling my hand to my chest protectively.

"I'll take Rusty's blood sugars," Shelly said. In one quick motion she put the pen to

my finger and clicked. In a moment a drop of blood was on the glucometer, and numbers began to flash.

"That looked easy," Jessica said, grinning at me. "Any fool could do it."

"Then you'd be perfect for the job," I said bitterly, picking up the pen and handing it to her. "Check your own blood sugars, OK?"

The smile disappeared from Jessica's face. "*My* blood sugars?" she said. "You're the sicky. There's nothing wrong with me."

Shelly tightened her lips and drew her eyebrows together. "Actually," she said, "it would be appropriate that you have your blood sugars checked. Any relative of a diabetic is at an increased risk for diabetes themselves."

"What!"

"That's right," Shelly said. She removed the old needle from the pen and slid a new needle into place. "So why don't we just have you take your blood sugars, and then we can put your parents' worries at rest."

"My parents aren't worried," Jessica said. She took a step back and attempted a weak smile.

"Actually, I am a bit concerned," Mom said, turning to face Jessica. "So let's just check things out while you're here."

"Mom!"

Shelly reached over and began to wipe Jessica's finger with a washcloth. Jessica backed up another step, but Dad reached out with a big arm and pulled her back toward the bed.

"It's easy," Dad said. "Any fool can do it."

"Here," Shelly said, pressing the pen into Jessica's hands. "All you do is push the end of the pen up against your finger and snap this button here."

"There's nothing wrong with me!" Jessica insisted. She held the poky pen straight ahead of her, her eyes round.

"Put the pen here," Shelly instructed. She maneuvered the girl's hands until the pen pressed against Jessica's middle finger. "Now, just give this button a little push."

"I'm not pushing any button," Jessica said, her voice rising.

Dad reached forward and gave the button a jab.

There was a loud *click* as the pen snapped shut. Jessica let out a shriek and jumped into the air as if she'd been bitten by a rattlesnake.

"That hurt!" she yelled.

"Hold still," I ordered, turning the glucometer on. "We need to get a drop of blood onto this machine."

But when we all looked at Jessica's finger,

there was no drop of blood to be found. "It poked me," Jessica assured us, squeezing her finger.

"So why isn't there any blood? I always knew you didn't have a heart," I said with a smirk. "I guess we shouldn't be surprised if you don't have any blood, either."

"You probably didn't have the pen pushed against your skin firmly enough," Shelly said, checking Jessica's finger herself. "That can happen sometimes. Especially with men who have really thick skin."

"It still hurt," Jessica said. She rubbed the end of her finger gingerly.

"Well, I guess we should try again," Shelly said. But this time she couldn't hold her smile back.

Jessica shrank back into Mom's arms. "No," she said. "Please don't poke me again."

"Well, I guess we'll let you off this time," Shelly said. She began to gather the equipment up. "I don't have any more time to spend here. But Rusty, I want you to notice something. It's much easier and more comfortable if you take your own blood sugars than if you have someone else do it for you. That's because you'll soon learn how hard you have to push the pen into your finger. It's bad enough being poked once, but if you have to

be poked twice it's really awful."

Both Jessica and I nodded our heads in agreement.

When Shelly was gone I pulled the lid off my tray and studied my dinner. It was boring again. A cheese and tomato sandwich, a bowl of mushroom soup, and a banana looked back at me from the tray.

"Don't I get dessert anymore?" I complained, taking a bite out of the sandwich.

Mom shook her head. "Weren't you listening to the talk today, Rusty?" she asked. "Diabetics can't have much sugar."

"No more desserts?" I asked. "Ever?"

A vision of chocolate bars and cheesecake and other treats passed before my eyes.

"Diabetics can have treats now and then," Mom said. "They can have a piece of cake at birthday parties, and they can have treats at Christmas. But they shouldn't eat anything sweet on a regular basis."

"It will be a tough sacrifice," Jessica said, "but I'm willing to eat Rusty's share of dessert. Because I love him, you know."

When my family left I flopped back on the bed with a sigh.

Seeing Jessica squirm had been the only good thing in an awful day. A dreadfully boring lecture on diabetic diets. A total flop when

it came to taking blood sugars. And now I was beginning to realize that diabetes was going to take a lot of the good-tasting things out of my life.

I'm going to ask You one more time, God. Take my diabetes away. I don't want to have to go through this anymore. And if You don't listen to me, I'm going to do something drastic.

I didn't know what I was going to do, but I figured something would have to happen. And soon.

12

ONE SMALL STEP FOR MANKIND

I opened my eyes the next morning with a smile. Evan was talking in his sleep again, but it didn't matter. I was going home today.

Tonight I'd sleep in my own bed. Evan's talking wouldn't bother me anymore. Mind you, I'd have Jessica, and that was bad enough. I think that Jessica could even out-argue Evan if she needed to.

I'd have real food to eat when I got home. The vegetables would be green, and the potatoes would be mashable—and no one would complain if I had pizza now and then.

Home, sweet home.

"I didn't do it, Pop," Evan said. His voice was loud again, and I pulled the pillow over my head, trying to ignore him.

"No! No! No!" Evan yelled. "Don't!"

"Be still!" I muttered.

"I'm gonna break your head open if you don't smarten up," Evan said. Then he was quiet, and I finally removed the pillow from my head and stared up at the ceiling.

Poor Evan. He was a jerk, but I had a feeling that his family were jerks, too. Wouldn't it be horrible if my family was like that? Never coming to see me, and not caring about my problems?

Lo, I am with you alway, even until the end of the world. God, You didn't help me at all, I thought, sinking back into gloom. *I thought You were supposed to help the people that You love. But here I am. My diabetes hasn't gone away. And I guess it never will. God, I was planning to really love You if You'd make me better.*

A tight feeling filled my chest when I realized what I had just thought.

That was it, wasn't it? I had been trying to force God to do what I wanted. I was holding back my love until He did things *my* way.

God, I was planning to really love You if You'd make me better.

Shouldn't I love God even if my diabetes didn't go away? God promised that He'd love *me* always, no matter where I was or what was happening in my life.

Well, I guess by now I can be honest with you. I'm pretty tough, I'm smart, and I'm a

good hockey player. But maybe—just maybe—I haven't been the best Christian in the world. I haven't really been a friend to God.

I told you that God had seemed to be like a fairy godmother to me, someone to wave a wand and solve my problems. Now I could see that it was a lot more complicated than that.

God loved me. Me! Craig Michael Hill, who wasn't always very lovable.

Sometimes I talk too much. Sometimes I show off and think of myself before I think of others. Sometimes I don't go out of my way to be nice to people, especially people like Evan and Jessica.

And I throw innocent cats down the basement steps.

There, I admitted it. I'm not perfect every moment of the day.

And God still loves me.

God, show me how to love You like that in return.

I didn't hear a voice. A beam of light didn't open from the sky and shine on me. But I had the strongest impression that God had a plan for me.

Love Evan for Me.

Love Evan? That would be too much. Evan wasn't lovable. My cat was more lovable than

Evan. My cat was smarter than Evan. My cat even smelled better than Evan.

God, I want to be a better person for You. I'm sorry for all the things I've done wrong. Thank You for loving me anyway. If it's Your will, please heal my diabetes. And if it isn't Your will, then please help me be brave.

If I have to have diabetes, then help me stop being scared. I have one more day to learn about blood sugars from Shelly. Help me to use this day wisely.

And help me to be nice to Evan. Because if this diabetes doesn't kill me, being nice to Evan might!

Don't ask me why I had this sudden change of heart. It doesn't sound very believable to me, so I suppose it won't to you, either. But that's the strange thing about real life. Sometimes it doesn't seem very real.

I just knew that God could make a difference.

I had tried to do it on my own, and I hadn't succeeded.

I could hear Dad's voice that evening when Ryan Smith had come to our house. He had been explaining to the men why he had decided to follow God and give up his career in professional hockey.

"I want to follow God's will in my life," Dad

had said. "Hockey won't always be there. But God will."

Today it seemed real. Hockey wasn't here. Mom and Dad and Pumpkin weren't here. Jessica wasn't here (that was a good thing, though).

But God was.

And God could make a difference in my life.

In a moment I discovered that someone else was here, too.

Miss McDonald.

It wasn't Shelly who walked into our room when Evan had me ring so he could use the bathroom. It was Miss McDonald.

She smiled when she saw me. "Why, Rusty, I thought you'd have been discharged by now."

"I get to go home today," I said quickly.

"Isn't that wonderful!" she gushed. "Now stay put. I'm going to run out and get my equipment so we can check your blood sugars."

This was too cruel.

I mean, I had just committed my life into God's hands, and in walks the only person in the hospital who's more scared of needles than I am.

Miss McDonald didn't fool me anymore. *Her* hand shook when she poked my finger. *Her* voice quivered when she gave me my insulin.

I stood up. This time all of my body was in

agreement with my fingers. We needed to get out of there, and we needed to get out of there fast!

I pulled my shoes on quickly.

But where could I go to get away from Miss McDonald?

There was a sudden loud bang behind the curtain and Evan began to yell. "Great!" he hollered. "Just great! I dropped the bottle. Can you pick it up for me, Rusty?" Evan asked. "I gotta go real bad."

"Didn't you go yet?" I asked.

"Of course not," Evan said. "Don't worry, you're not going to get your precious little chicken fingers dirty. Just grab me the bottle, OK?"

I hesitated. I could run. Of course, it wouldn't do me much good. Even if I escaped Miss McDonald, I couldn't escape my diabetes. I needed my blood sugars taken, even if I didn't actually want to be poked. That was the only way to tell how much insulin I needed.

And just a few minutes ago I had asked God for two things: to help me be brave, and to help me be kind to Evan. Well, here was my chance to allow God to work in my life.

So I shuffled back behind the curtain and crawled under the bed to find Evan's bottle. He didn't even thank me when I passed it to

him, but at least he didn't yell, either.

And when I came out from behind the curtain Miss McDonald was waiting for me.

"There you are, sweetie pie," she said. "I was beginning to think you'd disappeared into thin air."

If only it were that simple.

She handed me the washcloth. "Pick a finger," she said. "Any finger."

I grabbed the cloth and began to wipe my fourth finger carefully. *Help me be brave, God.*

Miss McDonald took my finger in her big hand and held the pen to the tip. "Just a little mosquito bite," she said. "I'm *so* sorry if it hurts."

I looked at the pen. She had it pointing straight at the tip. I remembered what Shelly had taught me. It would hurt more if I was poked on the very end of my finger like that.

I shifted slightly, but Miss McDonald kept the pen pressed against me firmly. "Hold still, young man," she said brightly. "Just a wee mosquito bite."

Suddenly I pulled with all my force, jerking my hand out of the nurse's grip. "I can do it myself," I said.

Miss McDonald's face showed surprise, but she didn't argue with me. Instead she passed me the pen with a look of mixed relief and doubt.

140

I took a deep breath and moved the pen to the side of my finger. *I can do this,* I thought. *Please, God, help me do this.*

My fingers trembled as I slowly reached my thumb toward the button. *Push the button,* I ordered myself. But nothing happened.

I tried again and again. And still I couldn't quite snap the pen into my tender skin.

Finally Miss McDonald let out a deep sigh. "Oh, that's just too bad, darling," she said. She sounded as disappointed as I felt. "You're so close, but you just can't do it. Here, let me help." She reached her chubby hand forward.

I hit the button. There was a sharp *snap,* and, when I looked, a perfect drop of blood formed at the end of my finger.

Miss McDonald stepped back and let me move the drop of blood onto the tip of the glucometer. In a moment the numbers began to flash, and soon the machine beeped.

"Six point three," Miss McDonald said matter-of-factly. "Very good."

She disappeared from the room, and I used a tissue to wipe the last of the blood from my finger.

I had done it! I had done it all myself!

And it hadn't seemed to hurt as much as it had before. Maybe Shelly was right. Maybe it did feel better if you did it yourself.

I got to go home that afternoon.

I hadn't realized how wonderful our house looked. There was Pumpkin, waiting patiently on the couch for me. He tried to play it cool by stretching and yawning when I came into the living room, but he didn't fool me.

Pumpkin was glad I was home.

I told you Pumpkin was kinda dumb. But he was loyal, too.

I guess I'm dumb sometimes, too. And dense.

It took me a long time that winter to learn that God had a plan for me. Maybe even Miss McDonald was part of the plan, because to be honest I doubt I would have taken my own blood sugar that day if Shelly had been there.

But she hadn't been, and things worked out for the best.

I've managed having diabetes better than I had thought possible. I've been out of the hospital for a month now, and I still wish God would take my disease away. But it hasn't been as bad as I had imagined it would be.

I can do my own blood sugars without any problem at all. Maybe my fingers have gotten callused, I don't know, but the pokes don't seem to hurt anymore. I told you I was tough. I've even started giving myself insulin in the belly. That's going OK, too.

I don't think I've done as well as I should in loving Evan. I pray for him every day, and I also pray that God will help me to be kind. It hasn't been easy, though.

Evan's still stuck in bed with his leg up in traction. His doctor told him he'd be there for a few more weeks, and then he'd need a full body cast.

A full body cast! Can you imagine? Evan says that means he'll be covered from chest to toe with plaster of Paris. "They don't cast my other leg, of course," Evan said. "And they leave a big hole in the back so I can go to the bathroom."

He laughed.

I had to laugh, too.

A sudden loud yell down the bedroom hall-way interrupted my thoughts. It was Jessica. "Craig Michael Hill!" she screamed. "You've been using my hairbrush."

"No, I haven't," I called back with a grin.

"You have, too!" she shrieked.

"Haven't."

"Listen!" she screamed. "My brush is full of bright-orange hairs! Short orange hairs! Doesn't that sound a bit like you?"

I smiled and stroked Pumpkin's side. It did sound a bit like my hair, I have to admit. It also sounded a bit like Pumpkin's.

"You didn't want to shed on my new shirt, did you, Pumpkin?" I cooed softly to the big cat.

He grinned back at me and dug his claws into my leg.

Dumb cat. Strange how I love him so much.

Dad and I have been to the hospital almost every day to visit Evan. Evan's parents have visited only once so far, so Evan is glad to have some company. Even if it's just a big McChicken like me.

Last night Evan even asked Dad to pray for him. "Not that I think it will do any good," he had said, "but if God can bother helping someone as chicken as Rusty Red Head here, then maybe He can bother helping someone terrific like me."

Mom's making homemade pizza tonight, and she's making an extra one for Evan. And we're going to take him a strawberry milkshake, too. One with real fruit.

Thank You, God, for loving me—even when I'm not very lovable. Or very smart. Please watch over my friend, Evan, and help him to learn to trust You. Like I finally do. Amen.